Hard to Get

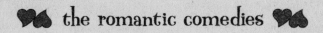
the romantic comedies

Hard to Get

EMMA CARLSON BERNE

Simon Pulse

New York London Toronto Sydney

This book is a work of fiction. Any references to historical events, real people, or real locales are used fictitiously. Other names, characters, places, and incidents are the product of the author's imagination, and any resemblance to actual events or locales or persons, living or dead, is entirely coincidental.

SIMON PULSE
An imprint of Simon & Schuster Children's Publishing Division
1230 Avenue of the Americas, New York, NY 10020
First Simon Pulse paperback edition February 2010
Copyright © 2010 by Emma Bernay
All rights reserved, including the right of reproduction in whole or in part in any form.
SIMON PULSE and colophon are registered trademarks of Simon & Schuster, Inc.
For information about special discounts for bulk purchases, please contact Simon & Schuster Special Sales at 1-866-506-1949 or business@simonandschuster.com.
The Simon & Schuster Speakers Bureau can bring authors to your live event. For more information or to book an event contact the Simon & Schuster Speakers Bureau at 1-866-248-3049 or visit our website at www.simonspeakers.com.
Designed by Ann Zeak
The text of this book was set in Garamond 3.
Manufactured in the United States of America
10 9 8 7 6 5 4 3 2 1
Library of Congress Control Number 2009936202
ISBN 978-1-4169-8951-6
ISBN 978-1-4391-5625-4 (eBook)

For H. B. B.—the best reason
to keep writing

Acknowledgments

Sincere thanks and appreciation go to my agent, Michael Bourret, who took a chance on me when he didn't have to, and to my editor, Michael del Rosario, for his keen and witty insight. Writing this book has been a yearlong journey I never would have completed without the unswerving support of my husband, Aaron. Thanks also to him for paying the bills. And Henry—thank you for brightening so many days when I stumbled blearily from my computer to rest my eyes on your chubby little face.

Hard to Get

One

This is the longest night of my entire life. I rolled over in bed for the millionth time, opened one eye, and squinted at my bedside clock. 3:00 a.m. I groaned, kicked off the blanket, and fanned some air under the sheet. *Just relax. Think nice thoughts.* Okay, nice thoughts. Cookie-dough ice cream. Sunbathing. Road trips. Boys with green eyes. Kissing. Kissing!

"Arrghh!" I thrashed around as the image of Dave kissing Taylor Kilburn flashed through my brain once more. I clawed at my pillow, wishing it were Dave's face instead. Again the scenario from last week played itself out in my mind. It was like some grisly highway accident you can't help staring at, even though you know you really shouldn't look.

After coming home last Monday, I realized I had forgotten my chem text and had to drive back to school late in the afternoon to get it. That's when I saw them. I remembered the bang of the metal door against the brick wall of the high school. Myself emerging, squinting in the bright sunlight, text clutched in my arms. Dave's car parked in the middle of the empty parking lot. My heart leaping. I thought he had come to pick me up. My lifted hand wilting halfway through the wave as I recognized *two* figures in the front seat. My feet rooted to the ground like weeds as I stared openmouthed at the heads bent close to each other. Dave's face turning toward me, his eyes wide. My frantic, stumbling retreat back into the deserted school.

Now, with one violent motion, I threw off the covers and climbed out of bed. I tugged at the window. The creaky wood stuck and then gave slowly with a screech of protest. I leaned out into the cool night air. "You're a giant jerk, Dave!" I shouted into the silent suburban night. "Do you hear me, you cheating stinkwad?" My voice echoed across the neatly fenced yard. Far away, a dog barked in response. I couldn't tell if he agreed.

I leaned my head on the window frame. How could I have been so wrong about Dave? I had totally misjudged him—and I never did that. And why *Taylor*? Former beauty pageant contestant who was never without her MAC foundation and plum lip liner? Did he actually like that kind of thing? Apparently so. I slowly rapped my forehead against the glass. Judging from the way his face was mashed into hers, he liked that kind of thing a lot.

Dave and I had been together since last summer, my longest relationship so far. Everything had seemed perfect. He was smart, cute, athletic, funny—all the things I wanted in a boyfriend. It was true he'd been a little distant ever since we got back from skiing at his parents' cabin over spring break, but I'd assumed he was busy with classes, like me.

Oh yeah, he was busy. I slammed the window shut and climbed back into bed. *Just not with classes.* I pulled up the tangled sheet and stared at the clock.

3:25 a.m.

The next morning I blearily inventoried the train wreck staring back at me in the mirror. Pasty skin. Dark circles under the eyes. Sleep wrinkles across one cheek. I took a few futile swipes at my hair, gave up, and threw it into a messy bun on top of my head. Eyes still mostly closed, I plucked my favorite old jeans from the back of my desk chair, where I'd thrown them the night before, and pulled on a navy blue tank top. So what if I looked like dog meat? It wasn't like I had a boyfriend to impress.

I grabbed my messenger bag and clattered down the back stairs. The yellow-painted kitchen was full of steam. Mom was standing at the stove, frying scrambled eggs with her glasses all fogged up.

"Oh, Val, is that you?" she said, turning her head in the direction of the doorway. "I can't see a thing. You want toast?"

"Mom, I totally don't have time. I'm late and——" I was interrupted by a familiar beep from outside. "See, there's Becca and Kelly." I grabbed the orange juice out of the fridge and took a quick chug from the carton. Luckily, Mom was still temporarily blind. I stuck the juice back into the fridge

4

and bolted out the door and down the porch steps. "Bye!" I bellowed behind me.

Becca's little red BMW purred at the curb, gleaming in the warm early-spring sun. Fall Out Boy was blasting from the open windows. I tossed my messenger bag into the back and climbed in after it.

Becca twisted around in the driver's seat. "God, Val, what have you been doing, beating yourself with a stick all night? You look like leftovers." She pulled away from the curb at about sixty miles an hour and sped down the street, fishtailing slightly.

Becca, on the other hand, looked like she'd been up since five. Her pink button-down shirt was ironed and her khaki shorts actually had creases down the front. She shook her head and her shiny black hair caught the morning sun. I scowled at her and tried to stuff a few strands into my bun with my fingers.

Kelly, her tan, muscular legs propped on the dashboard, whacked Becca on the arm. "You are so mean! I'm sure Val does not look—" She turned around and glanced at me. "Wow. You do look like leftovers."

I slumped down and rested my head on the back of the seat. "Hey, give me a break. I'm functioning on like two hours of sleep here. I was up all night reliving the humiliation of the year, courtesy of David Strauss."

Kelly nodded sympathetically, tying her blond-streaked hair into a ponytail. "You need to forget him. He's slime. You did the right thing dumping him like that after seeing him with Taylor."

"Right!" Becca chimed in. She slammed on the brakes, just managing not to rear-end the car in front of her. "Move on. He's totally not worth thinking about for one more second."

"Yeah, I know," I mumbled.

In the front seat, Kelly was rummaging in the giant sports bag on her lap. "Damn!" she said, emerging from the depths and blowing her hair out of her eyes. "I forgot my goggles. Becca, go back."

"Are you kidding?" Becca said as she flicked on the turn signal. "It's ten minutes until first bell and we've been late once already this week. No way."

"I had to borrow Madeline's yesterday. She's going to be mad if I mooch off her again," Kelly whined.

I stared out the window at the manicured

lawns and neat frame houses gliding by. Kelly played about eighteen hundred sports, so lost goggles and ripped volleyball shorts were standard fare during the daily rides to school. My thoughts drifted. Of course Becca was right—I *should* forget Dave. I'd dropped him out of my life, but it wasn't so easy just to drop him out of my mind. I'd never been humiliated like this before. I'd never even been dumped.

Becca broke into my thoughts. "I posted those pictures from the 10K last weekend, by the way."

"Oh good, we can see Val trying to run on her twisted ankle," Kelly said.

"Hey, I had to finish, right?" I said, perking up momentarily. Even in excruciating pain, I'd still managed to place in my age group.

"You were crazy!" Becca told me. "I can't believe you didn't just stop. I mean, come on—three miles with an injury?"

I grinned. "*You* can't believe I didn't stop? You should know me better than that after ten years of friendship."

"Yeah, Becca," Kelly said. "Remember who you're talking to. The freaky girl who is completely incapable of quitting anything she's started? The one who has to be the best at *everything*?"

"Not everything," I replied. "Just almost everything. I wasn't perfect at going out with Dave, right?"

"*He* cheated on *you*!" Becca exclaimed. "Don't start blaming yourself, or I'm never going to talk to you again. I don't know why you're stressing so much about him anyway. I mean, I'll admit, you guys *were* cute together, but it's not like you have to worry about finding another guy."

"Yeah, yeah," I muttered, climbing from the car and hoisting my messenger bag over my head and shoulder.

"You guys want to go for subs at lunch today?" Kelly asked just before we parted ways at the school entrance.

"Definitely," Becca replied.

I nodded. "Yeah. I need something to look forward to this morning."

Becca put her arm around my shoulders and gave me a squeeze. "Don't worry, chick," she said. "You'll find a new boyfriend by the end of the day today."

I forced a smile and headed off to my locker. Becca was right, of course. Dave and I had had a good thing, but he turned out to be a jerk, and now it was over. Time to just move on. But for some reason, the thought of finding someone new just made me feel like running out of the school screaming.

I headed down the long row of lockers, each with its combination lock hanging neatly from the latch, my thoughts clanging around in my head. *If you don't want a boyfriend, then what do you want, Val?* I asked myself as I reached number 381. Automatically, I reached for my lock and started spinning the knob. My brain took a minute to compute that something was off. I looked down at my hand. The lock was already open. And my locker door was cracked about an inch. I froze. I looked left and right. The hallway was deserted. I tried to peer into the crack without touching the door, but all I could see was the dark interior. My heart was beating a little too quickly. Did bombs ever get planted in high school lockers?

This was ridiculous. I couldn't stand here all day, staring at my locker. The bell was going to ring any minute. A few kids trickled into the hallway at the far end. Taking some weak comfort from their presence, I gingerly opened the door.

Several large soft objects tumbled off the shelf, landing at my feet. I jumped back and stared in disbelief. Instead of the usual jumble of books, scarves, sunglasses, and random pieces of paper, the entire locker was crammed with stuffed animals, red and pink boxes of candy, and cards in big pastel envelopes.

I bent down and retrieved a stuffed polar bear from the floor. A little red tag dangled from his arm. *Hey, Val, what's up? I figured out your lock combination—1-13-94—your birthday. It's my new favorite date. Hey, let's hang out sometime. Doug.* The hallway was starting to fill up. I edged closer to the locker door, trying to shield its contents from the stares of people passing nearby. A blond girl spun her own combination a few feet away and looked over at me curiously.

I shot her a weak smile and did my best to kick some of the stuffed animals back into the locker. I set the polar bear down and picked up a dog wearing a cowboy hat. He stared at me with benign button eyes. I extracted a card from the envelope strung around his neck. *From Justin.* I placed the dog next to the polar bear and pulled out a stack of candy boxes of various shapes and sizes, flipping through them as if they were a stack of playing cards. Heart-shaped box of truffles from Travis Gosdin, chocolate-covered cherries from Brian North, big bag of M&M's with VAL printed on them from someone named Randolph, Whitman's Sampler from Jason Goldfarb. Oh my God, this was just flat-out creepy. Is this what it feels like to have a stalker, I wondered? Or a lot of stalkers?

The warning bell rang. I snapped out of my trance. I had to get rid of this stuff before anyone saw it and thought I'd been flashing people for Mardi Gras beads or something. A jumbo-size trash can with a fresh garbage bag stood empty just a few feet away. I thought about dragging it over, but the second bell chimed and the halls began to empty. No time. I started cramming everything back into the locker instead. I was in the midst of trying to close the door while holding the stuff in with my foot when two people came strolling down the hall toward me. Oh, joy of joys—it was Dave and Taylor, *holding hands* and looking like Longbranch High's Cozy Couple of the Year.

Don't look, don't look. I concentrated on shutting the locker door, but it wouldn't close. Out of the corner of my eye, I could see two sets of shoes approaching—Dave's Reef flip-flops and Taylor's white strappy wedges. I shoved the locker as hard as I could, but something was blocking the door. I looked down. A furry little arm was poking out the bottom. The shoes stopped beside me.

Slowly, I raised my eyes and was hit smack in the face by Taylor's best beauty-pageant grin. "Hi, Val!" she chirped.

Unbelievable. Just unbelievable. I offered a tight little smile in return. "Hi. Hi, *Dave*," I said.

Dave cleared his throat. "Uh, hey, Val," he said uncomfortably. His face was patchy with red and I could see him trying to squirm his hand out of Taylor's. No luck though—she had it in an impressive death grip.

Taylor wasn't done turning the knife yet. "So, what's up, Val?" she burbled.

I gritted my teeth. "Nothing. Just trying to get to class." I gave the locker door another futile shove.

"I think there's something stuck in there," Dave said, oh-so-helpfully. He pointed to the bottom of the locker, where the furry arm still stuck out like part of the world's smallest murder victim.

"Oh yeah." I managed to sound surprised. "I don't know what that is." I held the locker door shut with my foot. If I let go, it would spring open and reveal the bizarre collection inside. On the other hand, would that be such a bad thing? At least he'd see that I was in demand. I wavered and, for an instant, released my hold on the locker latch.

"Here, I can get it." Dave stepped forward and grasped the latch. I realized what he was going to do.

"No, Dave, don't, I can—" I tried to yank his hand away, but it was too late. Dave opened the locker, and once again, stuffed animals and candy boxes sprayed all over the hallway.

There was a brief, horrible pause as the three of us surveyed the carnage. Taylor's eyes widened. Dave's forehead was wrinkled as if he were trying to understand a really, really hard math problem.

"What's all this stuff, Val?" Taylor bent down and picked a red stuffed heart off her sandal, turning it over in her hand as if it were an archeological specimen.

I summoned my courage. This was a test of my inherent toughness, kind of like my pioneer ancestors crossing the Rocky Mountains in the dead of winter and running out of food and having to eat one another by the end.

I tossed my head. "Oh, nothing." My voice held just the right hint of careless airiness. "Just some presents from a few . . . *friends*." I picked up the cowboy-hat-wearing dog and held him next to my cheek lovingly.

"I had no idea you were so popular," Taylor cooed. I resisted the urge to put my hand on her face and push her away. Dave stood by her side, his hands hanging like hams, looking from one of us to the other.

The warning bell chimed again. "Well, I've got to get to class," I said casually. I waited until they had retreated down the hall, then shoved the stuff inside, slammed the locker door, and rushed down the hall, in my haste almost ricocheting off the last row of lockers. I could feel the blood pounding in my forehead as I slid into my seat in English. *A week and a half! Whatever happened to a decent period of mourning?*

The classroom was filled with the soothing rustle of paper and notebooks and the low hum of people getting ready for the discussion on *Hamlet*. I took out my phone to turn it off for class, glanced at the screen, and then looked more carefully. Did that say *twenty-five* texts? I scrolled through the list fast. Matt, Rob, Aaron, Mike. Did I want to hang out; get some coffee; watch movies some night; come to a house party; hey, there's a barbeque this weekend, did I want to go?

I clicked my phone shut and laid my head on the desk. What was the deal? I mean, a couple of invites, maybe, I could understand, since everyone knew about the breakup by now. But twenty-five? And all the stuff in the locker? When had my life become so weird?

TWO

"All right, everyone, let's get started," Mr. Fleming said from the front of the room. I focused my eyes, temporarily distracted from the drama that was my life. Mr. Fleming was new at Longbranch, and already the entire female population had a crush on him. There was a rumor going around that he was gay, but who cared when he looked like he belonged in an Abercrombie catalog, not sitting sideways at a stupid high school desk, shuffling papers, like he was now?

"Before we plunge into our discussion on the role of the Ghost in *Hamlet*, I'd like to pass back your midterm papers," Mr. Fleming said. I straightened up. I'd worked for two solid weeks on my discussion of the character of Orsino in *Twelfth Night*. It was definitely one of the best essays I'd written. Mr. Fleming retrieved a stack of papers and began strolling up and down the aisles.

"Here you go, Val," he said, dropping the paper on my desk. "Nice work."

I stared at the stapled pages sitting in front of me. B+! How was that possible? I'd slaved over that thing! Furiously, I grabbed the paper and started poring over the red-ink comments in the margins.

"I want to remind everyone that there is a revision option for this paper," Mr. Fleming said, standing once more in front of the class. "If you do substantial revisions, I will gladly regrade the paper, up to one full letter grade. Revisions will be due in a week."

I did some fast calculations in my note-book. Right now my GPA for the class was 3.9. But with an A+ on the paper, I could get it up to 4.0 for the semester. I put down my pencil. I'd just have to revise. It didn't matter that this was the only B I'd pulled down all semester. I never quit something I've started, not if there is even the tiniest chance I can do better.

The discussion of the Ghost dragged. My other morning classes also seemed way longer than usual. Finally, the fourth bell rang and I closed my calc text with relief. Time to meet the girls for lunch. I needed some sustenance.

I slung my bag over my shoulder and made my way into the hall along with the river of other juniors flowing out of the classrooms. People were pressing up against me from behind as everyone surged toward the bright sunshine streaming in from the front entrance.

I had my hand on the push bar of the big double doors when I sensed someone behind me. I whirled around to see Kevin, Dave's most obnoxious, beery friend, leering at me. Kevin made a lasting impression by puking in the umbrella stand during my homecoming party.

"Hey, Val," he said, breathing like a rhinoceros. A miasma of musty aftershave hung over him in a cloud.

I tried to keep my nostrils from flaring with disgust. "Hi, Kevin. What's up?"

"Hey, I heard about you and Dave," he said, laying a hand the size of a steak on my shoulder. "And you know, if you ever want to hang out sometime, I bet I can make you feel much better."

Oh my God, he did not just say that.

I started backing into the doors, my polite smile rapidly deteriorating into a grimace. "Kevin, thanks for the, um, offer . . ."

He followed me. "I'm having some people over on Saturday. You want to come? It's going to be wild."

His face was looming larger and larger as he leaned toward me. "Maybe, thanks, Kevin," I choked out before I yanked my shoulder out of his sweaty grasp and pushed the double doors open. I caught a glimpse of his startled expression before the heavy metal doors banged shut.

I could see Becca and Kelly sitting in the car as I hurried across the asphalt. "Oh my God," I gasped as I collapsed into the backseat. "You would not believe my morning."

"Why? What happened?" Kelly asked as Becca pulled out of the parking lot with a screech. We had to rush if we wanted to get to the sub shop and back in time for the sixth bell.

"Oh, nothing, if you don't count the Valentine's Day explosion in my locker, twenty-five texts, *and* Kevin Daugherty almost jumping me in the hall just now."

Kelly looked over at Becca and nodded. "Told you."

"I know," Becca said.

"What?" I asked, leaning forward. "Told her what?"

Kelly flipped down the sun visor and rearranged her ponytail in the mirror. "I told Becca everyone at school would be talking about you. You're the Magically Single Girl."

"Thanks a lot," I said, flopping back in the seat. "I knew I could count on you for unconditional support."

Kelly reached back and patted my knee. "Anytime, girlfriend."

I set my tray on the table and slid into the booth next to Becca, unwrapping my turkey on whole wheat. "What is that, a lettuce sandwich?" I asked Kelly, eyeing her anemic meal.

Kelly looked slightly defensive. "There's a piece of cheese on it. I need to shed a few pounds before regionals." She took the top bun off her sandwich and discarded it. Becca rolled her eyes.

"So, did you guys hear that the theme for prom is Magical You?" Becca asked.

"Yeah. I think it's better than last year. I mean, Wonderful Tonight? Did they think it was 1978 or something?" Kelly said.

I put down my sandwich. In all the mess over Dave, I'd totally forgotten about the junior-senior prom in May. Of course, the last time I thought about it, I'd just assumed I already had the best date in the world. *Hah.* So much for that. My stomach started churning at the thought of Taylor prancing around the dance floor at the Belton Banquet Club with Dave clutched in her pointy little nails.

"So do you think Logan will ask you?" Kelly asked Becca. Logan was Becca's regular make-out buddy. They had a good system—no guilt, no commitment. They'd have marathon make-out sessions in Becca's den, and then go get tacos.

Becca nodded. "Yeah, I think so. He was kind of hinting at it the other night. You know—as long as it doesn't make us official. What's Brent been saying?"

"He keeps insisting he's going to wear a powder blue tux, but I told him that if he does that, I'm going to go in my Speedo."

I heaved a gusty sigh. Both girls looked over at me. There was a pregnant pause and then Becca said, "Don't worry, Val. You can go with anyone you want."

"That's the problem," I said, stealing one of Becca's potato chips. "I *wanted* to go with Dave. Obviously that's not going to work now."

We all chewed thoughtfully for a minute. I swallowed my bite of turkey. It tasted like glue. "Whatever," I said. "I've got more to worry about than prom. Dave's licking Taylor's face every day in the halls, I've somehow become a Happy Meal for all the single guys at school, *and* I totally forgot that the deadline for the community service projects is next week. Mrs. Masterson was talking about it in class again. I really don't want to do that group food-bank project. Maybe I'll do the individual option."

"I totally forgot too!" Becca exclaimed. "What are you going to do, Kel?"

Before Kelly could answer, I was distracted by a tap on my shoulder. I turned around. Willy Pearce was standing behind me, looking like he was ready to pass out. I could already hear the girls starting to snicker. Willy had had a crush on me for years. He was one of those guys who look like they've spent their entire lives in some dark basement. As he stood there, his pale blue eyes blinked nervously and his hands twitched. A few strands of blond hair were pasted to his forehead. "Uh, hi, Val," he finally whispered. It seemed to take all his strength to get the words out.

I kicked Becca under the table to stop her now audible giggles. "Hi, Willy. What's going on?"

"Oh, nothing," Willy said with a ghastly attempt at suavity. Silence descended. Willy's mouth worked but nothing came out. I waited patiently, rolling my sub paper into a little ball. "I—I was just wondering if maybe, um, maybe, if you're free, I could IM you one night and . . ." His voice gave out.

I groaned silently. "Um, sure. No problem. I mean, I'm really busy these days . . ." I shot a warning glance at Kelly, whose face was growing dangerously red. Chortles were escaping in explosive puffs from the corners of her mouth. "But we can IM sometime."

A wobbly smile spread over Willy's face and he rushed away, almost crashing into the trash can on his way out.

I turned to my friends, who had lost their restraint and were collapsed on each other's shoulders, weak with laughter. "See, what'd I tell you?" I said. "Val the Happy Meal."

Kelly rattled her straw against the bottom of the cup and sucked up the last of her Sprite. "Yeah, that's what you said in the car."

"I know. It's so irritating." I tried to shoot my balled-up sub paper at the trash can. It missed by several feet.

Next to me, Kelly raised her arms over her head and shot her sandwich paper at the trash can too. Of course, it went in. "I don't know, I think it sounds cute. I mean, all of these guys basically want you. Why is that irritating?"

I opened my mouth to respond but Becca held up her hand. "Stop! We have to go back or we're going to be late. To be continued—my house after school."

We all stood up and collected our bags. "I think we're playing basketball in gym next," Kelly said happily as she pushed open the smeary glass door.

"Ohhh," I moaned. "I totally forgot. Oh, God. I didn't bring my shorts." Ms. Lenning, the hyper-fit, hyper-alert gym teacher, was adamant about gym clothes. I'd already forgotten my shorts about fifty times this semester. Last time, she told me that if I left them at home one more time, she'd give me a D. Not that a D in gym really mattered, but it would drag down my GPA. Naturally, I couldn't let that happen.

"You can borrow mine," Kelly offered. She smiled at me and slid into the front seat as Becca started the engine. "Shotgun."

"Really? That would be great," I said, distracted from her poaching of the front seat. Luckily I still had an old pair of sneakers in my locker from the earth science class creek-walk.

"I don't know *why* you guys opted to take PE this semester," Becca sniffed. She turned onto the main road, lined with squalid strip malls and faceless Old Navys and Targets. "It's not like you have to."

"Hey, we can't all convince the guidance counselor that spinning classes at the Y are the same as a gym credit." Kelly propped her feet on the dashboard.

Becca glanced over. "For the hundredth time, could you please not do that? My windshield has all these nasty, smudgy toe prints all over it."

Kelly reluctantly thumped her feet to the floor.

"Yeah, how *did* you swing that one?" I asked, leaning forward between the seats.

"You've got a study hall and I'm stuck throwing balls of various sizes around with Dave and Taylor for company."

"At least that's your only class with them." Becca glanced in the rearview mirror. Her brown eyes were concerned. "Are you going to be okay?"

I tried to smile reassuringly. "Sure! I'll be fine." My voice came out a little overloud. I saw Becca and Kelly exchange glances.

I sighed. "Look, I made it through the morning, right? And things surely can't get any worse than that."

"Look at that, three minutes to spare," Becca said, turning into the school parking lot.

"Yeah, when you drive ninety," Kelly mumbled.

Becca ignored her. "Look, Val, everything's going to be fine. All those guys are just a little worked up about you being single. I'll bet they've forgotten all about it by now."

"And Taylor's probably totally irritating Dave already," Kelly chimed in. She hoisted her duffel from the floor of the car.

I smiled. "Thanks, guys. You're both terrible liars—but thanks." We climbed out of the car and Becca gave me a hug as Kelly practically bounded over to the doors leading directly to the gym.

"Come on, Val!" she yelled over her shoulder. "Bell in three minutes!"

I dragged myself after her. She hauled open the big blue metal doors, and the sweaty-foot, dirty-sock smell of the gym wafted out from the yellow-lit interior. I could hear the echoing thump of basketballs being tossed around, interspersed with staccato shouts.

Inside, most kids were assembled in slouchy groups on the bleachers, while several enthusiasts, including an already-sweating Kevin, were already racing up and down the court like they were playing in an NCAA tournament. Ms. Lenning, clad in her usual crisp white polo shirt and ironed green gym shorts, was ticking off names on the attendance sheet. With a nausea-inducing pang, I spotted Dave and Taylor sitting practically in each other's laps in a top bleacher. I looked away fast and followed Kelly to the locker room, which was mostly deserted and strewn with discarded jeans, T-shirts, and flip-flops. Kelly dug into her bag and tossed me a pair of shorts.

"These are tiny!" I held the minuscule garment up in front of me. "I said shorts, not underwear!"

Kelly sat down on one of the wooden benches with a thump and pulled off her jeans. "They're just my track shorts, that's all. I don't like all that fabric when I'm trying to run."

"No, I guess you like your butt cheeks hanging out the back instead," I mumbled, trying to squeeze the shorts over my hips. I wiggled right and left and finally got them up, just as the locker room door banged open.

"Anyone not on the court in ten seconds gets an F for the day!" Ms. Lenning hollered in at us. Without glancing in the mirror, I yanked on my T-shirt, sprinted for the door, and slid onto a bottom bleacher just as the bell rang.

Kevin spotted me after I sat down. "Val! Val! Hey, Val!" he yelled, skidding to a halt midsprint and waving at me like a two-hundred-pound cheerleader. Brian North and Travis Gosdin turned around too. "Hi! Hi, Val!" It was like a chorus of baby birds, except not babies and not birds.

I offered them a weak smile and twisted

around to see if Dave had noticed my popularity. But I couldn't tell because Taylor was now sitting directly in his lap, completely obscuring his face with her thicket of blond waves. I clenched my nails into my palms in hopes that the pain in my hands would distract me from the pain in my heart.

"Teams, everyone!" Ms. Lenning ordered. "Captains are Dave and Kelly."

Oh, God. I licked my lips, which were suddenly parched. Dave climbed down and stood in front of us. His sun-streaked light brown hair curled around his forehead and ears, and his big, sexy shoulders pushed against the thin fabric of his T-shirt. He looked so hot, I felt like crying all over again. Involuntarily, I twisted around. Taylor saw me looking and waggled her fingers at me with a smirk. I bit my tongue.

Kelly got off the bench and went to stand next to Dave. She raised her eyebrows at me. "You're on my team," she mouthed. I closed my eyes and offered up a tiny prayer: *Please, God, let Kelly pick first. I can't stand watching him pick* her *over me*—again. I surreptitiously picked at my tiny shorts, which had an uncomfortable way of wedging themselves where they weren't invited.

"Dave, you can pick first." Ms. Lenning waved her clipboard at him.

He didn't even pause. "Tay," he said with a big cheesy grin.

I coughed. Tay? Did he say Tay? I looked around for a place to vomit but, unfortunately, found none. Taylor, however, stood up, offered the assembled gym class her very best beauty-pageant smile, and skipped neatly down the stairs. I morosely watched her giant blond ponytail bounce by.

"I choose Val," Kelly announced.

I stood up. A murmur ran through the bleachers. Kevin's eyes grew wide. For a moment, I couldn't figure out what was going on. Then I saw Kelly's face, which had an apologetic grimace around the mouth. Our eyes met. *What?* I mouthed. Her eyes pointedly traveled downward. I glanced at myself. Oh my God. The shorts. They seemed to have shrunk even further since I put them on five minutes ago. The hem barely reached the bottom edge of my underwear, revealing my entire thigh and—I gingerly passed a hand behind me—a good portion of my rear also. I looked around. Brian North and Travis were nodding and grinning appreciatively. As I watched, Brian leaned over to another guy next to him and whispered something. The guy looked over at me and grinned also.

Ms. Lenning seemed oblivious. "Okay, come on, Val, get down here!" she shouted. "Dave, pick."

I didn't hear who Dave picked next because, as I walked over to Kelly, a slow clapping began behind me, and then spread, with more and more people joining in until the entire male population of the class was applauding my tiny shorts with sincere and genuine appreciation.

I gritted my teeth and forced myself to stand up straight. The clapping died down but the grins and nods didn't. With one exception—after a quick glance, Dave was ignoring me. I don't know whether that was good or not—he wasn't paying attention to my humiliation, but then again, he wasn't paying attention to *me* either. Instead, he was leaning over, clasping one of Taylor's hands as she whispered in his ear.

After everyone was picked, Ms. Lenning blew her whistle, and the squeak of sneakers and the thump of the basketball filled the gym. Almost immediately, I forgot about the shorts, Dave, Taylor, my life. Kelly grabbed the tip-off and wheeled around. Taylor was right in her face, but Kelly darted to one side and dribbled past her. "Kelly!" Maya Kohli stood under the basket, open. I raced over to them. Travis blocked Maya.

"Here!" I waved my arms. Kelly gave me a little nod and passed the ball to me. The rough leather *thunk*ed into my hands. I wheeled around but Taylor was guarding me now. She danced in front of me, panting, her mouth glistening. Our faces were so close, I could see a poppy seed caught between her two front teeth. Her breath smelled like watermelon Jolly Ranchers. I gritted my teeth and resisted the urge to just throw the ball at her head. Instead, I feinted left and right. Clear, I raised the ball to my chest and bent my knees to shoot. But just as my feet left the ground and the ball left my hands, a voice screamed behind me, "Don't worry, Val! I got it!" Then a massive, sweaty bulk slammed into me.

"*Ooof!*" Kevin's elbow hit me square in the diaphragm. The ball flew from my hands. I landed on the waxed wood floor and skidded several feet on my rear, coming to rest against the lower bleachers.

"Oh wow, sorry, Val." As I sat on the

floor, struggling to breathe, Kevin's concerned face loomed above me like a red moon in orbit. I looked up at him, and a large droplet of sweat fell from his forehead. It splatted right between my eyes. I opened my mouth and drew in a giant, shuddering breath. Kelly knelt next to me and patted my back.

"All right, nothing to worry about." Ms. Lenning's crew cut appeared behind Kevin's head. "Just got the wind knocked out of her."

"Val!"

"Are you okay?"

"Do you want me to take you to the nurse?"

"Do you want *me* to kiss it and make it better?"

A crowd of eager male faces clustered above me. Travis Gosdin reached down and tried to haul me to my feet by the armpits, while Brian North dusted off my barely clad rear, oh so helpfully.

"I'm fine," I snarled, swatting his hand away.

"I was just trying to help you, Val." Kevin crouched down next to me, worry pasted all over his big moose face. "I thought maybe you couldn't get that shot." He paused. I could see his brain working very, very hard. "But I guess I knocked you over instead."

"Right. You did." I struggled to my feet with Kelly's assistance. Ms. Lenning slapped my shoulder.

"Go take a breather, Val. Back on the court, everyone. Hustle! Hustle!"

I made my way toward the bleachers, but after a few steps, I felt like someone was watching me. I turned around. Kevin, Travis, Brian, and about six other guys were all standing in a knot, apparently enjoying the little show my shorts were putting on for them. Dave, however, had reverted back to his default position and was glued back on to Taylor's face as they stood off on the sidelines. I scowled at my attentive audience as fiercely as I could. Kevin smiled and nodded as if I'd just thrown him a bouquet of roses.

With a sigh, I sank down on the hard wooden bench and pressed my ribs experimentally, trying to gauge what kind of a bruise I was going to have by tomorrow. Then Ms. Lenning blew her whistle. "Foul! Taylor shooting two!" She pointed to the foul line.

I leaned back and rested my arms on the bleacher above me. This should be good. There was no way she'd make it. Now maybe Dave would see what a ditz he'd wound up with. Taylor stood at the foul line and awkwardly dribbled a few times. Everyone watched as she fumbled and the ball rolled away. "Oops." She giggled as she picked it up and started dribbling all over again. She poised herself to throw, holding the ball way too high, practically against one shoulder, her elbows almost over her head. I couldn't help grinning. Then she threw the ball and my grin disappeared as I watched it swish through the net in a perfect arc.

"Yeah, Taylor!" Dave shouted and ran onto the court to grab her by the waist. Everyone else on their side applauded as he kissed her right in front of the basket. I slumped down, cradling my still-aching midsection, watching Dave swing Taylor around in his arms like she'd just broken a world record.

"Scoot over." Kelly slid onto the bench next to me. "I think that brought new meaning to the phrase 'crappy throw.'"

"But she made it," I pointed out.

"So what, when she looks like Little Miss Strawberry Patch taking a shot?"

I looked over at Kelly's grumpy face and nudged her with my knee. "Thanks."

She nudged me back. "Sure. I'll bad-mouth your enemies anytime."

Three

After school, we convened in the basement at Becca's. I flopped onto a giant leather armchair. I was in serious need of some self-medication in the form of Twizzlers and a giant Diet Coke. Kelly stretched out on the couch opposite and propped her feet on the arm. "Ah," she said, grabbing a bag of M&M's and putting it on her chest. "I love your basement, Becca."

"Me too," I agreed, looking around the big, airy space, complete with plasma TV and built-in sound system. Becca's dad owned the biggest chain of lighting stores in the state, so they were loaded.

"Any more stalking at school?" Becca asked, sitting down cross-legged on the thick gray carpet and sucking up some Diet Coke through a Twizzler.

I curled up in the soft leather cushions. "Did Kelly tell you about gym?"

She nodded. "Yeah, Kevin trying to save you and Dave making out with Taylor—"

"Yeah, yeah," I said, cutting her off. "I know what happened. I was there, remember? What I can't figure out is why I'm getting all of this attention *now*, when I really, really don't feel like it."

"Well, I've got it figured out." Kelly lined up a row of green M&M's on the cushion in front of her. "It's so obvious, I can't believe we didn't think of it earlier."

"Are you going to let us in on the brilliant explanation, or what?" Becca asked.

Kelly ate the first M&M. "Val's available." She put another M&M in her mouth and sucked on it noisily.

"That's it?" I asked. "I already knew that."

Kelly rearranged the M&M's into a circle. "No, there's more. Think about it: This is the first time you've been single for more than twenty-four hours since eighth grade. These guys are just trying to seize their chance with you while they still can."

I opened my mouth to disagree, but then closed it. Could that possibly be true? I mentally shuffled a series of past boyfriends as if they were a deck of cards. Then I laid them out. Kelly was right. I'd gone from boy to boy to boy with less than a week total of single life in the last four years. "Wow . . . ," I said slowly. "You're right."

"Well, it's kind of nice having your pick, isn't it?" Becca laughed. She cracked another Diet Coke.

I shook my head. "No, it's really annoying me! Isn't it enough that I have to watch Dave with *her* constantly? Now, just because I'm single, I have to fend off every available guy?"

Becca rapidly chomped another Twizzler. She looked like she was thinking about something.

"Isn't that like your tenth Twizzler?" Kelly asked.

"Isn't that like your ten millionth M&M?" Becca countered, shoving the last of the Twizzler into her mouth. "Do you want a lettuce sandwich with those, too?" She turned to me. "You need to escape, Val. Too bad you can't drop out for a while. If you had some time to hide out, I bet you could get over Dave *and* all the guys at school would forget about you."

Kelly sat up. "That's it! Val runs away to Jamaica! She grows dreads and starts living on the beach. Yah, mon!" She laughed so hard a green M&M flew out of her mouth and bounced off the flat screen across the room. She got up to retrieve it.

"That's the problem," I said, slithering off the chair. I curled up in the fetal position on the carpet. "I *want* to get away but I can't. Obviously, I'm not going to drop out of school."

"Plus, you'll never be able to avoid going out, not as long as you're at Longbranch," Kelly told me. "Look at your history. Duh."

"I need a break!" I insisted. "I don't *want* my locker looking like the circus escaped. I think what I need is to just be alone for a while. Like this," I said, my voice muffled.

"Well, you can stop dreaming now," Becca said. "You'd need to escape to another country if you want to get away from guys."

I heaved myself off the floor and grabbed my bag from the sofa. "I doubt my parents would let me relocate to France, so I don't think that would work. I have to go. See you guys tomorrow."

I let myself out of Becca's and thumped down the front steps. My feet carried me automatically through the wide, tree-lined streets and past the neat suburban houses. I barely felt the weight of my bag strap pressing on my shoulder as I turned Kelly's theory over in my mind. It *did* make sense—all the stuff in my locker, all the attention in gym class (little shorts aside), all the texts—but why were all these guys so obsessive? There were plenty of other single girls at school.

I turned onto my street and trudged up the winding walkway to our big gray Victorian. The overgrown yew bushes in the front mostly obscured the porch, but I stopped when I spotted a flash of red through the branches. There was someone on the porch. Mom and Dad weren't due home for another couple of hours. A Girl Scout? The neighbor looking for her cat again? I crept up to the steps and my heart sank. There were actually *two* someones on the porch.

"Hi, Kevin. Hi, Willy," I said with as little inflection as I could. "Why are you guys stalking me?"

Kevin stood up from the porch swing. He'd changed out of his sweaty T-shirt from earlier and was now wearing a navy blue polo. His hair was wet, as if he'd just showered. "What's up, Val? I just thought I'd come by and, you know, apologize one more time for the whole gym class thing. But then this buttface shows up. I don't know what he's doing here." He gestured to the opposite side of the porch, where Willy was perched on the railing like an elf, his arms wrapped around his updrawn knees.

"Hi, Val," Willy whispered. He hopped down from the railing, blinking his eyes several times in succession. "I brought my laptop so we could IM."

I shook my head. "But, Willy, you're right here. I'm talking to you. So we don't have to IM."

He looked crestfallen. "Oh. It's just that I thought you said we could IM, so I . . ." His voice trailed off.

I gritted my teeth. The beginnings of a headache were starting in my temples. "Well, we don't have to IM. Okay?" I said tersely. "We're talking right now."

He nodded silently. Still standing at

the bottom of the steps, my bag over my shoulder, I looked from Kevin's red, meaty face on one side of the porch to Willy's pale one. The door was in between them. I briefly considered making a run for it. Then I sighed. "Look, guys, I really don't know what's going on. All I know is that this has been the craziest day of my life. I'm so tired and I have a headache. I don't want to talk or"—I held up my hand as Willy opened his mouth—"IM." He closed his mouth. "Okay?" I mounted the steps and went inside. But as the door banged shut, a thought occurred to me. I turned around and pulled the door open. They were both still standing on the porch, exactly as I had left them.

"Can I ask you guys something?"

"Sup?" Kevin replied. He looked unfazed by my shutting the door in his face.

"Um, this might sound kind of weird, but . . . how come neither of you have ever asked me out before?" I couldn't believe I was saying this aloud, but I had to know if Kelly was right.

"Dude." Kevin sounded as if he couldn't believe how dense I was. "There wasn't any chance. You always had a boyfriend before."

Willy nodded in silent agreement.

"Thanks." I pulled the door shut again and leaned against it, exhaling only when I heard their slow footsteps leave the porch.

That night, after dinner, I retreated to my room to start working on the *Twelfth Night* revision. I flicked on Taylor Swift and climbed onto my bed, opening my laptop. It wouldn't hurt to check out Facebook for one second, just to see those race photos Becca posted. I clicked on my profile and rubbed my eyes as I stared at the screen. Did that say *forty* new friend requests? Maybe it was a computer glitch and there were actually four. I scanned down the list. No, it was forty. All guys from school. I ignored every one, poking at the keyboard so hard I jammed a knuckle.

Focus, Val. I closed out of Facebook and found the *Twelfth Night* paper in my folder. I scanned the comments. Mr. Fleming thought the opening was weak. I opened my *Complete Shakespeare* and poised my fingers over the keyboard. Suddenly, Viola's first line in the play caught my eye: "What country, friends, is this?" Viola was shipwrecked in Illyria, a place she didn't know and where no one knew her. I tapped my fingers on the page, thinking. Viola's life was totally new. She could do anything she wanted. How awesome would that be?

Suddenly, I sat up. Shakespeare slid onto the carpet. Wasn't that kind of what Becca had been saying earlier? Escaping. *What if I pulled a Viola?* I jumped up and paced restlessly around the room, stopping to stare sightlessly out the window. I couldn't run away of course, but what if I just . . . checked out for a while?

I sank down on my bed, thinking hard, and then clicked open my chat window. Luckily both Becca and Kelly were online.

Me: *Girls, are you there? This is going to rock your world.*

Becca: *What's up?*

Kelly: *My world could use a little rocking. I hate calc problem sets!*

Me: *I've been inspired by Shakespeare. Are you ready?*

Becca: *Just tell us already!*

Me: *I'm going to pull a Viola.*

Kelly: *You're going to pretend to be a guy?*

Me: *No, I'm going to escape for a while.*

Becca: *What are you talking about? Your parents will freak out if you go to France.*

Me: *No, I'm not going to France. I'm swearing off guys!*

Becca: *What are you talking about?*

Me: *No boys and no romance. Isn't this brilliant?*

Kelly: *I'm not sure "brilliant" is exactly the word. "Insane" might be better.*

Me: *Thanks for the vote of confidence. Let's meet for breakfast tomorrow. I'll explain the whole thing.*

I closed my chat window. This plan could save my sanity and, hopefully, the rest of my junior year. But first I had to figure out the details.

Four

"I would've asked for this in a sippy cup if I'd known you were going to be driving the Saab," Becca said the next morning as we headed for the Sunporch Café. She attempted another sip of her caramel latte just as I wrestled the car into second. A wave of amber liquid baptized her Seven skinny jeans. "Val!" she exclaimed.

"Hey, at least we even have a car to drive today," I said, fighting with the clutch. "Mom was threatening to take it grocery shopping, but I talked her out of it." At the next red light, I remembered to press the clutch before stomping the brake and gingerly easing the Saab into neutral.

"Yeah, I feel *so* lucky the Beemer's in the

shop," Becca muttered. She had a blob of whipped cream on her upper lip. It made her look like a transvestite Charlie Chaplin. "How come we're not picking up Kel?"

"She's meeting us. She wanted to bike." The light turned green and I took a deep breath. Foot on clutch and brake, then off brake and on clutch, shift into first, press on accelerator, then foot off clutch but carefully. A fire truck began wailing just behind me and roared past as I slammed my foot on the brake, forgetting the clutch, of course. "Darn!" The Saab jolted across the intersection in big bronco bucks.

"Hel-help, hel-help," Becca jerked out, holding on to her coffee with both hands.

"Hang on, I've got it now," I said, just as the motor stalled.

"Val, get us out of here!" Becca yelled, staring at the line of cars forming on either side of us. I could hear a few ominous honks.

"I'm trying!" I forced myself to breathe before I shifted into neutral again and carefully eased into first. Bing. The Saab crept smoothly across the intersection as if it had never stalled in its life.

"So," Becca breathed. "Are you going to tell me about that madness online last night?"

I grinned. "No, wait until we get there. Then I can explain it to both of you at once." I braked hard as the green awning of the Sunporch suddenly loomed in front of me. The car slewed sideways and wound up in a parking space, bumper first. "Hey, look, right in front!" I chortled as I climbed from the car. I recognized Kelly's bike locked to the telephone pole in front of us.

"You're three feet from the curb!" Becca protested. She stared at the wide gap of asphalt in dismay.

"Whatever! Let's go, I'm starving." I could see Kelly waving to us from a table in the window. "I need some eggs Benedict, like right now."

The steamy fragrance of frying bacon hit me full in the face as we pulled open the glass doors. Sunlight flooded the little restaurant, pouring in the big front windows and spreading in pools on the gleaming wooden floor. All around was the pleasant murmur and clink of breakfast, punctuated by the ring of the cash register up front.

"Okay, talk, you," Kelly ordered the moment we slid into our seats. Her wet hair was pulled back in a loose braid, and her skin was fresh and rosy. Three orange juices stood at our places.

"Oh my God, please don't tell me you've already been running," Becca moaned as she opened the huge plastic-covered menu. "It's ten o'clock on Saturday!"

Kelly shrugged. "I only did five miles like usual."

Becca rolled her eyes and looked up as a waitress with a shaved head and big plastic plugs in her earlobes appeared by our table. "I'll have the banana chocolate-chip pancakes with whipped cream, a side of bacon, and two eggs, scrambled. Thanks."

"Just oatmeal for me and a grapefruit," Kelly said. "And coffee with skim milk."

Becca's glare practically burned a hole in the booth behind Kelly's head. "You know, I think I'll have a side of hash browns also," she said to the punked-out server.

Kelly smiled sweetly. "Actually, no milk with the coffee. Black is fine."

I sighed. Another morning with passive-aggressive food competition. "Eggs Benedict," I said. The waitress nodded, blank-faced, and scribbled on her pad before walking away.

"Okay!" Kelly turned to me like a woman on a mission. "Talk, crazy lady."

I grinned and took a leisurely sip of orange juice. The girls leaned forward across the table.

"Come on!" Becca said. "You're driving us crazy. What was the deal with all that weird stuff about Violet?"

"Viola," I corrected. "Remember, the girl in *Twelfth Night*?"

They both stared at me blankly.

"See, Viola gets shipwrecked and she's all alone, so——"

"Whatever!" Becca cut me off. "Are you out of your gourd?"

I leaned back in my chair. The sun streaming in the window was warm on my face. "I'm one hundred percent sane. It's just like I said. I'm swearing off guys."

"Forever?" Kelly asked.

"No, just until school lets out. It'll be the perfect end to my junior year. For the first time since eighth grade, there'll be no boys in my life at all. I mean, not romantically. It's a brilliant plan. "

Kelly snorted. "It would be brilliant *if* you could hold out that long. School's not out for two months. You won't even last *one* month."

"I can too last a month!" I insisted like a five-year-old.

"You can't."

The flat finality of her voice irritated me. "Kelly Meade, I can." I was getting loud.

"So do it." She widened her eyes at me.

"Fine," I snapped. "One month." I fixed her with my eyes. She stared right back.

Becca pursed her lips. "What about flirting?"

I shook my head. "No flirting."

"What about just *talking*?" Becca asked.

I thought. "I guess talking is okay. I mean, like my chem lab partner is a guy and I have to talk to him. And telling Willy I can't go out with him, that would be okay."

"Right," Kelly said. We were silent a moment, and then she burst out laughing.

"What?" I asked.

"This is impossible! You won't be able to do it. For one thing, no one can go a whole semester without at least *flirting*." She pointed her coffee spoon at me as if it were a fencing sword. Little brown droplets dripped off it.

"Well, I can. Have a little more confidence, will you?"

The waitress arrived with her laden tray and set down our food. I took a bite of my eggs Benedict. The hollandaise was silky and delicious.

"Is this all because of Dave?" Becca asked, pouring half a pitcher of syrup over her pancakes.

I cut into my second egg and watched as the yolk ran over my plate. "Partly. But it's also everything that's been happening at school. All the stuff from guys is really getting on my nerves. Maybe checking out for a while would give me a new perspective on things." I speared a piece of Canadian bacon and stuffed it into my mouth.

"Well, it seems kind of out of character for you," Becca said. "You've *always* had a boyfriend."

I thought of Kevin and Willy on the porch yesterday. "So? A person can change, can't she?" I said, poking at another piece of egg. It slid out from under my fork and flew off the plate, landing on the front of Becca's pink cashmere sweater.

"Val!" Becca dabbed at the egg. "Look, sure a person can change. But why are you being so extreme? Why not just say, I'm not going to go out with anyone for a while? Why all the rules?" She dipped her napkin in her water and scrubbed at her sweater.

"Sorry about that," I said.

"Well, don't be sorry. I mean, I'm just giving you my opinion—"

"No! I meant sorry about the egg." I leaned forward. "And as for all the rules, I mean, I have to have a plan if I'm going to do this. If there aren't any rules, I might screw it up. And you guys know—if I'm going to do something, then I'm going to do it right. No half-assing." I waved my fork at them. "I thought you guys were my supportive friends, huh? Whatever happened to that?"

"We *are* supportive," Becca soothed. "It's just that this seems kind of . . ."

"Crazy?" Kelly suggested.

I heaved a disgusted sigh. "Look, just trust me. It's going to be great."

"Yeah, but this is totally out of character for you," Kelly insisted. "You wouldn't even know how to do it."

"Nuns do it all the time." Becca ran the last piece of pancake around on her plate.

"But Val's not a nun," Kelly pointed out. They both looked at me.

"Maybe you should think about becoming a nun," Becca said.

"Guys! I'm not becoming a nun. I'm just swearing off having a boyfriend. Like detoxing. I'm going to get it out of my system so I don't make another mistake like Dave." I looked from one skeptical face to the other. Then I slid my plate to one side and flipped over my paper placemat, dotted here and there with hollandaise. I extracted a pen from my bag. "All right. I can see you guys aren't convinced I'm serious." At the top of the placemat, I wrote *Val's Grand No-Boyfriend Plan*.

"What are you doing?" Becca asked. She craned her neck across the table.

"I'm making it official."

Number 1, I wrote. *No going out with anyone but friends. That means guys, girls, frogs, or princes.* I slid the paper around so the others could see.

Kelly read it and nodded. "So far so good."

Number 2, I continued. *No flirting—arm touches, cute smiles, hair tossing, etc. Number 3, No romance—no gifts, love notes, kissing, holding hands. This plan is binding for one month. I hereby swear to it.* I signed my name with a flourish and shoved it across the table.

Kelly grabbed it. "Wow, a contract! All right, Val, you're on." She folded the placemat and stuck it inside a library book in her bag.

"So when are you going to begin the GNBP?" Becca swiped her finger through the syrup pooling on her empty plate.

"GNBP?" I asked.

"Grand No-Boyfriend Plan."

"How about tonight?" Kelly suggested, a little smile curling the edges of her lips.

"But your house party is tonight," Becca pointed out. Kelly always threw the first party after we got back from spring break, and it was always awesome. Everyone from school would be there.

"So?" Kelly's voice was tough. She stared at me with one eyebrow slightly raised.

I stared back and lifted my chin. "Tonight's fine. Great, in fact. I was just thinking I should get started right away." I had actually been thinking I would give myself a couple of days to get used to the idea, but nothing annoyed me more than Kelly in a competitive mood.

Kelly smiled and looked out the window. I threw down my napkin and stood up. "I have to make a potty stop," I said.

I banged my way into one of the dented metal stalls in the gray-and-pink-tiled bathroom. Kelly could be really bitchy sometimes. Everything had to be a competition. The outer door opened. A pair of Doc Martens came in and went into the end stall. I could hear the beeping of a cell phone.

At the damp sink, I turned the water on full blast and pumped a pool of pink soap into my palm. I stared at my face, made pasty by the fluorescent light, in the spotted mirror. My eyes were huge and hollow and my hair looked glued to my head. I sighed and shut off the water. I wouldn't have any trouble with my No-Boyfriend Plan if I kept looking like this.

As I pushed out of the bathroom and threaded my way through the tightly packed dining room, I could see Kelly and Becca leaning toward each other across the plate-strewn table. I fell in behind our punked-out waitress as she approached the table with the check.

"—bet on it," Kelly was saying. "So do you want to do it?"

"Oh, fine," Becca said with a sigh. "I'm in."

The waitress set the plastic tray with the bill on the table and stepped away.

"What are you guys talking about?" I asked.

Their right hands were clasped together.

They both glanced up at me. Becca's cheeks grew pink.

"Oh, hey, Val." Becca removed her hand from Kelly's. "I thought you were in the bathroom."

"Well, obviously, I'm done now," I said, my hands on my hips. "Do what? Why were you guys shaking hands?"

"We weren't," Kelly said.

"You were, Kelly Meade. I saw you."

Becca sighed. "Just tell her, Kelly."

"Tell me what?" I perched on the edge of my chair.

"It's totally nothing," Kelly said. "We were just making a little bet. For fun."

Becca glanced at Kelly. I looked from one to the other.

"So? What were you betting on? Why are you acting so mysterious?"

"Well, if you have to know," Kelly said, "I was just saying that I bet you wouldn't be able to keep this GNBP going for a whole month."

"And *I* was saying you would," Becca chimed in. "So Kelly was just saying we should make a bet on it."

I straightened up. "Heck, yeah. We can bet on it. *If* Kelly's prepared to lose." I stared daggers at her.

She gazed back at me sweetly. "I'm never prepared to lose. That's why I don't."

"So what are the stakes? It better be good if I'm going to go to all this trouble. All-expenses-paid trip to Cancún? H and M shopping spree?" I gave her a toothy smile.

"Uhh . . ."

Becca spoke up. "I know exactly what the stakes are. And believe me, this is worth it. I'll show you guys tonight."

We all looked at one another. For a moment, no one spoke. Then I reached out my hands, one to each friend. "Okay. Let's do it."

"Yes!" Kelly pumped her fist in the air. "You're on."

We did a three-way shake to seal the bet.

Outside the café, a pale spring sky spread over the sun-warmed sidewalk and the hesitant scent of hyacinths drifted from a planter near the café entrance.

"So, you guys are coming over early tonight, right?" Kelly said. She dug around in her REI bag for her keys. "I'm making nacho dip."

"Wait, are you serious?" I asked. "After what happened last time?" The "last time" under discussion involved a food processor, several burnt pans, and the fire department.

"Look, I've perfected the recipe. It's going to be awesome." Kelly unlocked her bike from the telephone pole and threw her leg over the seat. "We'll order pizza for dinner. See you tonight!" she called over her shoulder.

"So you're going to start the GNBP tonight?" Becca asked as we climbed into the Saab.

I took a deep breath. "Yeah, I guess I am." I glanced in my side mirror and lurched away from the curb.

Five

Kelly barely glanced at us as she threw open the door that evening. She was wrapped in a towel and her wet hair streamed down her back. "Hey, hi," she said, whipping up the stairs. In her room, the bathroom door stood open, billowing clouds of steam. We could hear the shower running as she disappeared into the bathroom and banged the door shut.

Becca dropped down on the red-striped carpet and immediately pulled out her phone.

"Who are you texting?" I asked, grabbing a copy of *Vanity Fair* from Kelly's nightstand.

"Logan," she said, not looking up from

the screen. "He's thinking of going dancing tonight."

"Tell him to come here! There'll be plenty of dancing," I said, gazing at a picture of Robert Pattinson wearing a black leather vest.

"That's what I'm saying."

I could hear the shower shut off in the bathroom. A few minutes later, Kelly's arm reached out and pushed the door open a few inches. The smell of cucumber body wash wafted into the room. "So did you bring the stakes with you, Becca?" she called.

"Yep," Becca called back. She set down her phone and reached into her Kooba bag, next to her on the rug. As I watched, she pulled out a large blue velvet jewelry box. I raised my eyebrows and she grinned.

A blow-dryer started up in the bathroom. "Well?" Kelly shouted over the noise. "What is it?"

Becca didn't say anything, just smiled.

"Kelly, I think you better get out here for this," I said, my eyes still fixed on the blue box.

"Okay, hang on." The blow-dryer shut off and the door opened the rest of the way. Kelly appeared, wearing a pink bathrobe and holding a flat iron with a trailing cord. She plugged it in by the dresser and sank down cross-legged on the rug. "Enough with the suspense. What is it, Becca?" She pulled the iron through a section of hair.

"I think you have that up too high," Becca said. "It smells like it's burning."

"What is it, already!"

Becca flipped open the lid of the box. I gasped. There, glittering on a bed of velvet were the most gorgeous earrings and necklace I had ever seen. The earrings were diamond studs, from which dangled huge double hoops completely covered in pavé diamonds. Tear-drop diamonds hung from each center. The necklace was a thick silver chain with a massive tear-drop diamond pendant, surrounded by pavé diamonds. To my inexperienced eyes, it looked as if it were the size of a golf ball. Becca lifted the earrings out first. Each one had two interlocking hoops. When she held them up to the light, the hoops separated and rotated around each other, shooting off little glitters of blue, orange, and red. She laid the earrings on the comforter, where they shone incongruously on their background of faded red cotton, and placed the necklace carefully next to them.

"Those are not real . . . ," I said slowly. Becca nodded.

"They're totally real. Dad just opened up the safe-deposit box yesterday and gave them to me. Apparently they've been in there for years and he forgot about them." She got to her feet and placed her hands on her hips. "I propose that the person who wins the bet gets to wear this stuff on prom night. If it's you and me who win, Val, one of us will get the necklace and the other the earrings."

"Well, you'll have to wear them both," I said. "I'm not going to prom."

"What!" they both said in unison. Becca stared at me as if I'd just said I was going to change my name to Michelangelo and repaint the Sistine Chapel. "How can you not go to prom?"

I shrugged, trying to look as if I didn't care. "I don't see how I can. The GNBP isn't over until after prom. Remember? Prom's in less than a month."

"Oh, right." They fell silent.

"I know! You could go stag and meet us there," Becca suggested after a minute.

"I wouldn't be able to dance," I argued.

"No, you could dance with us. Just no

slow dances. It's the *guys* that are off-limits, not the dancing."

"That's true . . . ," I said slowly. "I don't know, though . . ."

Becca silently held up the earrings in one hand. The necklace dripped from her other. The diamonds glittered.

"Okay, I'll go," I said.

"Yeah!" Kelly cried. She threw her arms around me, then picked up the earrings and, moving over to the mirror in the corner, slipped them into her ears. She gazed at her reflection for a long moment, turning her head one way, and then another, then looked at us. "What do you think?"

"Wow," I said. "You look like Blake Lively at the Emmys."

She grinned and looked back at herself. "Okay," she said, taking the earrings out and laying them back on the bed. "It's a deal. Whoever wins gets to wear the bling to prom. But I think we're being a little too nicey-nice here, ladies. What about something for the person who *loses*?"

We considered this. "Okay, fine," I said. "What are you thinking?"

A wicked little grin spread across Kelly's

lips. Without answering, she crossed the room to her walk-in closet and flicked on the light. She went in, and Becca and I listened in silence to the rustling of fabric. Then she emerged with something large and purple in her arms.

"What the heck is that?" Becca asked. Kelly threw the bundle on the bed.

"Take a look," she said, pointing. I got to my feet and shook the bundle out. "It's a dress," I said, holding it up. "A—"

"Really, really ugly dress," Becca finished for me. We both stared at the thing like we were gazing at a nasty car accident. It was blindingly bright purple, with a long taffeta skirt that was held out stiffly by black tulle petticoats underneath. The bodice was high-necked, with more black lace around the collar. Long sleeves with giant puffy shoulders finished it off.

"I got it at the thrift store for last year's Halloween but I wound up going as Dana Torres, remember?"

"Vaguely," I replied, my eyes still fixed on the dress. It was so breathtakingly hideous, I just couldn't look away. "Are you saying . . . ?"

Kelly nodded. "Exactly. Not only does

the winner wear the diamonds to prom but the *loser* wears this."

I let the dress crumple back onto the bed.

"And these shoes." She threw a pair of matching bright-purple fake leather pumps onto the bed.

"Wait, what happens if Becca and I lose?" I asked. "There's only one dress."

Kelly frowned. "Yessss, that is a problem." She thought for a minute, tapping her finger on her cheek. Then her face lit up. "I've got it. One of you wears the dress for the first half of prom, and one of you for the second."

"This is serious," Becca said, prodding the taffeta mass with one finger.

"Isn't that the point?" Kelly had that challenging note in her voice again. She looked over at me.

I got to my feet. "You're on," I said immediately.

"Yeah!" she cried and held up her hands for us to slap.

Just then the doorbell rang downstairs. "Oh, hey, it's the pizza." Kelly started toward the door.

"I'll get it," I said, elbowing her out of

the way. "Last time, you ate half of it before it got to the kitchen."

Kelly's mom was weaving down the hallway, her usual martini in her hand. She smiled vaguely through her heavy black mascara. "Having a good time, girls?" she asked, looking past my left shoulder. A trickle of gin dripped onto the thick, cream-colored carpet.

I looked around in case some other girls had materialized behind me. "Yeah, great, Mrs. Meade." But she was already heading down the hallway, humming to herself, the martini glass tilting dangerously in her hand.

I paid the pizza guy and, balancing the half dozen hot boxes on my hands, headed for the kitchen. On the way back, I cut through the den. Kelly's older brother, Joseph, and a bunch of his friends were sunken deeply into the brown suede couches, playing Halo. The flickering blue and gray lights reflected off their intent faces in the darkened room. Joseph glanced up as I brushed by him.

"Hey, Val!" he greeted me enthusiastically. He slapped the cushion by his side. "There's a controller here waiting for you."

I took a deep breath. Here was a chance

to practice the GNBP before the official start. I always hung out with Joseph and the guys at Kelly's. He was pretty cute and we'd always had a little back-and-forth flirty thing going on, so this was perfect. With visions of the diamonds glittering from my ears, I arranged my face in a bland, neutral expression.

"Hey," I muttered. My voice sounded a little strangled. I tried to nod seriously as I edged toward the door.

The other guys glanced up. Curtis, Fuller, Laurence—all seniors, all the sexy soccer types, lean, blond, not too hairy. "Val!" Curtis yelled. "Get over here!" He reached out to pull me down on the couch next to him. I leapt back as if he was covered in lice.

"Whoa! Uh, hi, Curtis!" I backed away. "I mean, hi, Curtis," I said in a low voice. Did that sound flirty? I stood in front of them awkwardly, my hands dangling at my side. This was hard.

Joseph stared at me curiously. "Hey, is everything okay?" he asked. "You seem kind of . . .weird."

"What? No! Weird? I don't know what you're talking about," I stammered, trying to keep my face set in the serious, bland expression. I could feel my left eyelid beginning to twitch.

Now all the guys had stopped playing and were staring at me, the game controllers slack in their hands.

"Well, okay!" I said, backing toward the door. "Nice meeting you, Joseph. I mean, seeing you. Wait, um, no, it was *fine* seeing you." I laughed weakly. "Yeah, that's what I mean, fine. And you guys, too. Fine seeing you, too. Okay! Bye!"

I fled.

Safe in the upstairs hallway, I wiped my sweaty palms on my jeans and dabbed at the dampness on my upper lip. If that scene was a harbinger of my new life, I might not survive junior year. But whatever. That was only practice. I'd be fine.

By eight, everything was set. The pizza had been successfully guarded from Joseph and the guys, and Becca and I were stationed by the front door. I had decided I needed all the help I could get, so I was wearing my dullest outfit: plain gray T-shirt, khakis, no jewelry, flip-flops. No makeup, just ChapStick. I pulled my hair into a ponytail. When I looked in the foyer mirror, I almost fell asleep, I looked so boring.

Becca, on the other hand, looked like a dark-haired Gwyneth Paltrow or something. She was wearing a silky cream-colored tank top with a draped front, black capri leggings, and sequin-encrusted cream ballet flats. Giant silver hoops dangled from her ears, almost brushing her shoulders. I felt like a third-grader standing next to her.

"Oh my God, I'm so excited!" Kelly squealed from the top of the stairs. She was wearing a black tank dress and espadrilles that laced halfway up her calves, and of course, she looked amazing too, like those surfer girls who were always posing with their boards on the beach.

"Val, stop fidgeting," Becca said. She leaned closer to the hall mirror and swiped her lips with MAC Lipglass, carefully blotting the edges with a forefinger.

"I can't help it," I muttered, wiping my sweaty palms on my khakis for the millionth time. "This is going to be weird."

Becca looked at me in the mirror. "Don't chicken out, Val." Behind her, Kelly paused on the bottom step, listening.

"No, of course not," I declared, forcing

myself to stop fiddling with my ponytail. "You know I wouldn't do that. I haven't even started yet."

"Good," Becca said. She closed the lip gloss tube with a snap and tossed it into her bag.

"I don't know, Val." Kelly came forward. "It's hard to believe you're actually going to get through an entire night and not flirt with anyone, even *once*."

I swallowed. Just then, the doorbell rang. From behind the frosted glass of the door, I could see a cluster of shadowy figures. I took a deep breath. "Look, remember who you're talking to, girls. The GNBP is going to be awesome. And I'm in it to the end, of course."

"What's up, Val?" Brent yelled, as I opened the door. He and Logan stood on the porch, with a little knot of people behind him clutching bags of chips and six-packs of Coke. Brent stepped into the foyer and reached out to give me his usual bear hug.

I backed up quickly, bumping into Kelly, who caught my arm. "Hi, Brent." I kept my voice neutral, but my mind was buzzing. *Okay, Brent, let's see . . . Kelly's boyfriend. Attached. So therefore, not a GNBP threat. Okay to hug,* my GNBP computer advised. I reached out to hug Brent back, but he had already brushed past me into the living room. I must have looked confused because Kelly patted my arm.

"Okay?" she asked.

I nodded tentatively. Then I forced a big smile. "Fine!" I said brightly.

By eleven o'clock, Kelly's was packed with everyone I knew from school and a whole bunch I didn't. The Killers were wailing from the iPod dock on the coffee table, and Kelly's nacho dip—this time made without help from the fire department—was taking a serious beating. A huge red-faced guy yanked open the doors leading to the patio.

"Out of my way!" he yelled. He lowered his head and ran full speed through the doorway, pumping his arms like an Olympic sprinter. From my position by the drinks table, I could just glimpse the back of his shirt disappearing in a splash of water as he jumped, fully clothed, into the pool.

About two feet away, a couple I didn't recognize was stretched full-length on a wide leather sofa. The girl kept trying to kiss the guy's neck, but he was concentrating on stuffing chips into his mouth while lying down. I personally might find that a turnoff, but the girl apparently didn't. As I watched, she abandoned her efforts to give him the world's biggest hickey and instead focused on unbuttoning his shirt.

I turned back to the drinks table, which already looked like someone had driven a truck over it, and poked around for a clean cup, finally finding a few hiding under a pile of spilled corn chips.

"Val!"

I turned around. Kelly was standing behind me, clutching a bona fide Greek god by the sleeve. He looked like he could have been carved from marble.

"This is Craig," Kelly said. "He goes to Our Lady of Mercy."

"Wow, hi, Val." The god smiled devastatingly.

I wasn't sure exactly what the "wow" was for since I wasn't *feeling* particularly "wow," but hey, maybe this guy was into the boring look.

"Hey," I replied. I couldn't help smiling at him in return.

Kelly released the Greek god's arm as if planting him there and took a step back.

"Can I get you a drink, Val?" the god asked. He was standing so close I could smell his Acqua di Parma cologne. And let me tell you, it wasn't at all unpleasant.

"Sure," I murmured, looking into his eyes. I could feel a little smile creeping over my lips.

He reached over and gently took the plastic cup from my hand, then slowly filled it with Diet Coke from an almost-empty two liter. He handed the brimming cup of soda to me along with another blinding white grin.

"Thanks," I murmured, accepting the cup and automatically edging closer to him. I smiled into his big brown eyes. "Are you going to have a drink too?" I asked, raising my eyebrows a little and curling the edges of my mouth up in a way that never failed.

"Sure," he breathed.

Out of the corner of my eye, I could see Kelly standing a few feet away, watching the two of us intently and grinning widely. In the back of my mind, a little alarm bell rang faintly, but the presence of the living, breathing deity was just too distracting.

I sipped from the cup and then offered

it to the god. He was just reaching out his hand when a voice exploded in my ear.

"Hey there!"

I jumped and dropped the cup of soda, which splashed all over the Greek god's Diesel jeans, spreading a large wet patch over his crotch—a really unfortunate place for a stain.

"Crap!" he yelled, jumping back. Becca was standing next to me, apparently having shot up through the floor, breathing like she'd just run a 5K. She looked from the Greek god, now gazing hopelessly at his sopping pants, to me standing wide-eyed with my fingers still clutched in the shape of the cup.

"Val!" Becca exclaimed. "What are you doing?" She stared at me hard, her eyebrows raised.

"Uh," I stammered. "Um, doing?" Darn it! Three hours into the GNBP and I was already screwing it up. Next to her, Kelly had dropped the Cheshire cat grin and was mopily scraping dirty cups into a trash bag.

"Yes," Becca enunciated. *"Doing."*

"Oh! *Doing!*" I glanced at the Greek god. "Right. Um, nothing?" I bared my teeth at her ingratiatingly.

"That's right." She nodded, taking me by the arm. "Nothing is the right answer. Come on—look, C.J. has just gotten here and she's wearing the sluttiest shirt you've ever seen. Let's go laugh at her." She steered me across the room, then hissed, "What the heck was going on? If that wasn't flirting, then I'm Madame Curie."

"I know, I know," I told her, dropping onto the leather sofa, now vacated by the hickey couple. "I totally didn't even realize what was going on until you showed up. I was just going on automatic."

"You can't just *forget*," Becca emphasized, her eyes wide. "You have to get through a whole semester!"

"I *know*," I said.

She switched gears. "You're just getting started." She patted my shoulder encouragingly. "It'll get easier."

"Yeah. Or something."

Becca hoisted herself off the sofa. "I think Logan is getting lonely. Look, he's starting to fall asleep." I followed her pointing finger across the room to see Logan stretched out in an easy chair, his arms crossed on his chest and his eyes half-lidded.

"You'd better go rescue him," I said.

"I know. See you later." She gave my shoulder a squeeze.

I followed her figure across the room and saw her tap Logan on the shoulder, then bend down and whisper something in his ear. His eyes suddenly widened and a huge grin spread across his face. Becca reached down and pulled him up. They pushed open the patio doors. I could hear Becca giggling as they disappeared into the shadows next to the pool.

All around me, groups of people were dancing, talking, draped over furniture. Voices floated in from the patio. From the kitchen, I could hear the blender going and Kelly's voice shouting, "No, Brent! Not the guacamole!"

"Hi, Val," a masculine voice said near my ear. I jumped, knocking my funny bone against the couch arm.

"Ow! Hi . . . um, Randolph?" I massaged my throbbing elbow.

The pleasant-looking brown-haired guy in front of me nodded. "I gave you some M&M's? In your locker?"

"Oh, right . . ." I ever so slightly started scooting away from him. He sat down next to me on the sofa. Apparently, Randolph didn't take hints very well.

"So, I heard you broke up with Dave Strauss," he began, but before he could continue, a familiar figure approached from across the room.

"Hey, Val, I've been looking everywhere for you!" Kevin lumbered up, grinning and sweating as usual.

"Ah, hi, Kevin." I got to my feet and looked around the crowded room for the nearest exit. Groups stood everywhere, blocking my path to the door. Randolph frowned at the interruption. I started backing away, only to bump into the back of a guy standing nearby.

"Sorry," I mumbled. He turned around. It was Travis Gosdin, with Brian North next to him. Big smiles lit up their faces.

"What's up, Val?" they said in unison.

"I didn't even see you here before." Brian stuck his hand in his pocket and withdrew a crumpled piece of paper. "Hey, this is an invite to this dance my youth group is having next Saturday. Do you think you want to go with me?"

I opened my mouth, but before I could say anything, Kevin elbowed his way in front of me, his brow lowering dangerously. "Hey, punk, she's going to *my* party on

Saturday. Right, Val? The one I told you about in the hall?"

I looked from one face to the other. This situation was getting slightly out of control.

"I—um, actually, I'm not going—" I was cut off by a tug on my arm.

"Val," Randolph whispered. "I was going to tell you that our lake house is really amazing and—"

"Hey, who's talking to you?" Travis turned on Randolph, with Brian right behind. "Butt out, dude." His voice rose.

"*I'm* talking to Val here," Kevin bellowed.

"No, you're not, jerk-off." Brian faced him, his fists clenched. The other guys closed in with interest. I quietly edged toward the door, and when I was in reach, lunged for the doorknob and the sanctuary of the porch beyond.

Six

I pushed open the screen door and stepped out onto the porch. The cold night air was fresh against my cheeks after the crush of the house. I sank onto a cushioned porch swing, half-hidden behind a thick white pillar. I leaned my head back and gazed at the deep black sky, where a few inky clouds were scudding across the crescent moon. I closed my eyes. Dave's face reared up in the darkness behind my eyelids. He gestured to me apologetically and put his arm around Taylor, whose orange-painted lips were stretched across her teeth in a victorious grin. Together, they waltzed across my field of vision, smiling into each other's eyes. Then the rattle of voices nearby startled me out of my half doze.

"Dude, he was totally making out with her and she found them in the parking lot," a guy's voice was saying.

"She *saw* them?" a girl squealed.

I raised my head. A small group I hadn't noticed before was sitting in the shadows at the other end of the long, deep porch, perched on drawn-up chairs. I could see the tips of cigarettes glowing like orange pin-pricks in the dark.

"How awful," another girl breathed, her voice dripping with false sympathy.

I sank back on the cushions, wishing it were possible just to melt away and ooze onto the lawn. I might as well just parade the school hallways wearing a sandwich board reading THIS GIRL WAS JILTED BY DAVID STRAUSS. But then I'd be depriving everyone of such a fun opportunity for juicy gossip.

I leaned back farther in the porch swing, ignoring the creak of the chains, and curling myself in a tight ball. The creaks grew louder. Suddenly, I heard the sound of wood splintering and then the seat of the swing tilted up dramatically, dumping me backward, over the porch railing behind me and into a row of spiky yew bushes.

I yelped and thrashed around like an

impaled fish. Sticks were poking me every-where and the bushes smelled ominously of cat pee. "What was that?" someone on the porch said, and then there was a general scraping of chairs. I yanked at my T-shirt, which was snarled in a clump of branches. With effort, I stuck one leg out of the shrub and, grasping a branch just over my head, pulled myself out of the bushes. A row of faces appeared over the porch railing like a series of small moons. Any chance I'd had of hiding was now utterly gone.

"Hey!" someone said. I couldn't face a horde of gossipmongers right now. I fled around the corner of the house toward the backyard and skidded to a halt as I came in full view of the pool, now full of splashing juniors, including Kevin and Brian, who had apparently *not* killed each other inside.

Their backs were toward me but I could be spotted at any moment. I glanced around. A weathered gray trellis stood to my right, and on a sudden impulse, I darted behind it. I paused, panting. A stand of cypress trees created a thick piney wall that pressed against my back. I huddled against the prickly needles. At my feet, a narrow path of thick, mowed grass led back through the cypress trees. I'd never seen the path before, but then, I usually didn't spend much time lurking around the outskirts of Kelly's yard.

A group of girls, screeching with laughter, passed just a few inches away. Even though I knew they couldn't see me behind the trellis, I stepped back a few feet, then turned and, pushing through the branches, followed the path back into the shadowy, silent grove. Through a gap in the trees, I could see a sliver of the pool and the bright colored lights strung around it. The splashing and shouting voices were muffled, as if the party were much farther away than it really was. All around me, the cypress trees pressed thick and cool.

I followed the narrow path as it twisted around one tree trunk and then another, my feet leaving silvery footprints in the dewy dark grass. I was walking what seemed like an incredibly long way. I had to be off Kelly's property by now. I probably should go back, I thought, instead of wandering around randomly in the bushes like this. But the grass was so cool under my feet and the walking was soothing, like a massage.

Then I rounded a hairpin bend and gasped. There in front of me a perfect garden glowed like a little jewel set in dark branches. Mowed paths meandered among beds of rose-bushes, which hung their pink and red heads over the path, strewing it with petals. Banks of purple irises massed along the borders and the air was heavy with the fragrance of the wisteria intertwined in the arbors. The moon shone its eerie silvery light over everything.

I wandered into the deep shadows under one of the arbors and emerged into the moonlight again. I rested my palm on a mossy stone bench in front of me. The pitted stone still held the warmth of the day. I sat down and leaned back on my hands, letting the stillness drape over me.

Then a paperlike rustle disturbed the silence. I sat up on the bench and peered into the darkness. The moonlight clearly illuminated the paths, but deep shadows crowded the edges of the garden. I leaned forward. The rustle came again.

"Is someone there?" I called out. I guess I should have been scared but I just wasn't. This place seemed too magical for anything bad to happen. I tiptoed softly over the grass toward the rustle. I still couldn't see any-thing. I ducked under an arbor and bumped into something large and warm.

"Hi," a voice said.

I shrieked and jumped. "Who're you?" I squeaked, backing out of the arbor fast. He remained standing underneath it.

"Um, Adam," he said from the darkness. I heard the rustle of paper again.

"Why don't you come out here?" I suggested.

He stepped forward into the moonlight. Icy blue eyes and a shock of brown hair. He was tall and lean, wearing a faded blue zip-up hoodie that looked like it had been nibbled by mice and then run over with a truck several times, and a pair of canvas slip-on shoes.

"Hi," I said.

"Hi." His voice was surprisingly deep. "I'm Adam. Um, did I already say that?"

I giggled involuntarily. "Yeah, you did."

He grinned. "Sorry about that. I've been hanging out with my grandfather too much." He glanced around. "So what's a nice girl like you doing in a place like this?"

I groaned and rolled my eyes at the insanely cheesy line. "I could ask the same thing about you. How come you're hiding back here in this garden instead of at the party?"

"I *was* at the party until about half an hour ago," he said. "But the naked water polo was a little too much for me. I needed a break." He grinned. I noticed he had very white teeth.

I laughed. "I'm Val," I said.

Adam stuck out his hand. "Nice to meet you." His palm was hard and callused as it rasped against mine.

"So, do you go to Longbranch?" I asked.

"Yeah. I'm a senior."

I nodded. That explained why he didn't know me. Our school is giant, and he wasn't the type we hung out with anyway. He looked like one of those guys who took AP Drawing and Painting and spent a lot of time reading little books in the halls, or crouching over the developers in the darkroom. He did have nice eyes, though.

There was a little silence. Suddenly, I felt like we were standing too close, even though he was a couple of feet away from me. I took a step back. "This garden is amazing, huh?" I said, just to say something.

He glanced at the flowers all around us. "Yeah. It's a Shakespeare garden."

I blinked. "A what?"

"A Shakespeare garden. The guy who

owns the place is completely crazy for Shakespeare, so he made this garden like it would have been in Shakespeare's time, same flowers, everything. My dad's a contractor—he did some renovations on the house, that's how I know." He paused as if something had occurred to him. "Hey, what are *you* doing back here?"

"What? I, um, back here?" I fumbled, still caught up in the whole Shakespeare thing. What a weird coincidence. "Uh, just taking a break, you know. Getting some air. Heh-heh." I let out a weird little laugh.

But Adam didn't seem to notice anything strange. "So," he said, shoving his hands in his sweatshirt pockets. "You want to go back to the torture chamb—oops, I mean, party?"

I giggled and he grinned.

"Sure," I said.

He drew his hand out of his pocket, and at the same time, a piece of crumpled paper dropped to the ground.

"Hey, you dropped something," I said. I reached for it and cracked my forehead against his as he bent down at the same time. "Ow!" I straightened up fast, rubbing my head.

"Uh, thanks," Adam said, quickly reaching for the paper. "I got it—" His voice faltered as I smoothed it out. "That's nothing, just some scribbles . . ." I stared at the rough charcoal sketch. My own face stared back at me.

I looked from the sketch to Adam and back again. "This is me," I pointed out. He had drawn me in profile, my ponytail curling over one shoulder. I was leaning forward, my chin resting in my hands, flowers and vines swirling behind me. I looked up at Adam again. I wasn't sure whether to be flattered or creeped out.

Adam cleared his throat. "I was sitting here and I saw you come in but you didn't see me and you were sitting there on the bench, so . . ." He blushed. "I don't know. So I just sketched you. I don't know. Sorry." He held out his hand to take the paper back but I held on to it. He didn't seem that creepy, I decided, just shy and awkward.

"Can I keep it?" I asked. "No one's ever drawn a picture of me before."

His eyes widened. "Sure," he said.

"Thanks." I slid the paper into my back pocket. Then I noticed the purple swelling on his forehead. "You're getting a giant bump."

"So are you," he said. Only then did I feel the throbbing on my own forehead. I brushed my fingers over the hard swelling.

"It hurts," I confessed.

"Let's go get some ice for it," Adam suggested.

I followed him down the path toward Kelly's. Inside the house, the vast stainless-steel kitchen was deserted. I banged cabinets, looking for dishcloths, while Adam extracted ice cubes from the freezer.

I studied his hands as we held little matching bundles of damp blue-striped dishcloth to our heads. Long fingers, knobby knuckles. Then he shifted his grip on the ice and I noticed with a shiver that he was missing the tip of his ring finger on his left hand.

"So, what were you, an FBI informant in your previous life?" I teased. He looked at me, startled.

"What?"

I pointed at his missing fingertip. "That's a gruesome injury, I have to say."

He lowered his ice bundle and glanced at his hand. "Oh, that. Yeah, I was wearing a wire and the Mafia realized it."

I laughed. Adam grinned. "Um, yeah, I

sliced it off cutting mats last year," he said, dumping the ice in the sink and pitching the dishcloth on the counter. "It was great— I bled all over my junior project."

I shivered. "Ick. Did you freak out?"

"Yeah, it was kind of freaky. But I had a great excuse for postponing my calc final."

We laughed. Adam gently removed my bag of ice and inspected the bump on my forehead. My face tingled as his fingers brushed my skin and I suddenly thought of the GNBP. Was this a violation?

No, I decided, studying Adam as he turned away and opened the fridge. He'd taken his sweatshirt off and was now wearing a much-washed black T-shirt that read TWISTED SISTER. I never went for the self-consciously ironic retro hipster look.

"So, the soda's all gone, but there's, like, thirty different kinds of Arizona tea in here," Adam said, his head still buried in the fridge. He craned his neck around to look at me. "Want one?"

I nodded and sank down in one of the kitchen chairs. This day seemed like it had started a very, very long time ago. I'd just taken a gulp from the frosty bottle of peach-mango Adam had set down in front of me when the kitchen door swung open and Becca stumbled in. Her blow-out looked electrocuted and her eye makeup was smudged—of course, because it was Becca, instead of resembling a sloppy drunk, she just looked attractively tousled. "Val," she started to say. Then she stopped and glanced from Adam to me and back again. Her eyes narrowed. *"Val,"* she said pointedly.

"Bec." I widened my eyes and tried to subtly indicate *not a risk, not a risk.* Was she blind? Couldn't she see he was utterly not my type?

"I've been looking for you for an *hour*." Becca came over and tried to yank me up from the kitchen table.

"Hi," Adam said—politely, I thought, since Becca hadn't even acknowledged that he was sitting right there.

Becca turned and stared at Adam. "Hi," she said coolly. She turned to me. "Let's go. I totally forgot I'm supposed to take tickets at that tennis thing tomorrow morning."

"I can't believe you let your mom sucker you into another one of those," I said, rising. Adam stood up also.

"Maybe I'll see you around, Val," he said.

I glanced at him sharply but he had already turned away to dump our tea bottles in the recycling bin. "Yeah," I said slowly. "Maybe."

Seven

Becca glanced at me as we approached the front doors of school Monday morning. "You look kind of . . . pale, Val," she said. "Are you nervous?"

"Sort of. I didn't even eat breakfast this morning." I smiled at her and rubbed my sweaty palms on the side of my jeans. To help my plan, I was clad in another invisible-girl getup: a guy's V-neck white T-shirt, saggy jeans I usually wore camping, and Tevas. "This *is* the first official day of the GNBP, after all. My new life is waiting for me!" I sounded more brave than I felt. I eyed the entrance ahead. The doors had been chocked open to let in the warm spring air and I could see the lobby already filled with kids milling around, sitting cross-legged on the floor finishing homework, leaning against the walls, talking on their phones.

"But you started the other night at the party," Becca said.

"I know, but this is the first *real* day— you know, at school, a whole day, that sort of thing." I widened my eyes to impress on her the supreme importance of the occasion.

She patted my shoulder as we parted ways by the lockers. "Go get 'em, tiger. See you at lunch."

By second period, I was feeling more confident, despite my rumbling stomach. I found an invitation to Kevin's party on Saturday in my backpack, but even so, the invisibility outfit seemed to be working. I actually passed Brian North and Travis Gosdin in the hallway and they barely glanced at me. True, they were talking to each other at the time, but still, by the time I slid into my seat across from Kelly in calc, I was wondering why I ever thought the GNBP was going to be hard.

"How's it going?" Kelly asked, looking up from her phone.

"Great," I said, setting my messenger bag on the floor. "I feel really free, you know?" Something was weird about my seat, lumpy. I looked down. Tinfoil was sticking out from under my thigh. I shifted to one side and extricated a foil-wrapped bundle of something. Kelly raised her eyebrows at me.

"Ah, Miss Rushford, may I remind you that food is not permitted in class?" Mr. Henning pointed to the bundle. His long, red neck bobbed up and down like a reproving brontosaurus's. I picked up the package. A golden brown chocolate-chip cookie peered out through a gap in the foil. My mouth started watering.

"Sorry, Mr. Henning," I mumbled. I quickly sniffed the bundle. It smelled amazing. I flipped it over. *From Willy* read a scrawled label stuck to the bottom. Darn. Most definitely a GNBP violation. I looked up and smiled weakly at the boy himself, whose eyes were glued to mine from across the room. His hair was sticking straight up. When he turned his head, I could see the matted part at the back where he'd slept on it. Kelly leaned over to read the label and snorted.

"Tsk-tsk. Naughty, naughty," she whispered. I scowled at her. At the front of the room, Mr. Henning uncapped a marker with relish and turned to the whiteboard. Immediately, a soporific lull fell over the room.

"Let's take out our notebooks and begin with problem set six point four!" he bubbled, sounding as if he were really saying, "Let's take off our clothes and have a wild orgy!"

I stuffed the cookies under my seat and determinedly opened my binder, trying to ignore the delicious chocolate scent wafting up to me. Up at the whiteboard, Mr. Henning was enthusiastically solving problem set 6.4 all by himself. I glanced around the room. Ten people were texting, three were sleeping—one with his head on the desk—and five were staring blankly out the window. I picked up my pencil just as my phone vibrated in my pocket. I slipped it out of my pocket and glanced at the screen.

Do you like the cookies?

Oh, God. I snuck a glance at Willy. He saw me and a sloppy grin spread over his face, which was an alarming shade of scarlet. I ducked my head. Across the aisle, Kelly was doodling curlicues and spirals in her notebook and humming a little tune.

Me: *Yeah, thanks.*

Hopefully, that would get rid of him.

Willy: *It's my grandmother's recipe. I asked her to make them especially for you. They're hazelnut-dark-chocolate-raspberry.*

Did he have to tell me that? The aroma of chocolate was stronger than ever. In a minute, I was going to start drooling all over my problem set. I glanced down at the cookies. The edge of one was still sticking out. I could just break off one tiny piece. I was about to pass out from hunger anyway. As quietly as I could, I poked my fingers into the package, all the while keeping my eyes innocently on the whiteboard. The foil rustled. I froze and looked up. Kelly was staring at me fixedly. Across the room, Willy sat on the edge of his seat, apparently anticipating my first bite of Grandma's Aphrodisiac Cookies.

Suddenly, the realization of what I was about to do hit me. Day One of the GNBP and I was about to screw it up for a cookie. How could I do this? I summoned my resolve and, grabbing the cookies from under my seat, I reached back and tipped the whole package into the wastebasket standing against the wall behind me. Willy buried his face in his hands. Kelly stared at me a moment longer, then shrugged and returned to her doodling. I lay back in my seat, arms dangling, legs splayed out, heart hammering. At this rate, I wasn't sure I was going to survive to see senior year.

As I crossed the wide green lawn at lunchtime, I could see Becca and Kelly already sitting under our usual tree near the parking lot. I dropped my bag to the ground with a thud and sank down next to them. "Ohhh," I moaned.

"Is your arthritis bothering you again, Grandma?" Becca asked as she delicately ate cashews with the tips of her fingers.

"Give me a break. Calc was a little rough." I unwrapped my tuna sandwich and shoved half of it into my mouth with the first bite.

"Kels told me." Becca licked the salt off a cashew. "Poor Willy. He's probably headed for a life of drugs and misery and it'll be all your fault."

I tried to stick my tongue out at her but my mouth was full of tuna. I settled for throwing a baby carrot at her head.

Kelly took a swig of water from her Nalgene. "Hey, did you guys hear that

Taylor's getting her prom dress custom-made? Some place that makes wedding dresses is doing it."

Becca huffed. "Kelly, is it really necessary to have up-to-the-minute updates on the life of Taylor Slutmaster?"

"It's fine." I lay back on the grass, stuffing my bag under my head for a pillow, and crooked an arm over my eyes. "I'm totally, one hundred and fifty percent over it. I've moved on. On, on, on. On into the sunset, riding a white horse. Good-bye, Dave. Good-bye, Taylor. I hope you both get married and have lots of babies. Have a nice life together."

"Yeah, you sound really over it," Becca said. From the dark behind my eyes, I heard rustling and the crunching of what sounded like apple slices.

"Are you sure they're even going to prom?" Kelly asked.

I snorted. "Why wouldn't they? I'm sure Dave's got the hotel room all reserved and waiting."

"Ohhh! I cannot stand the idea of watching them hump each other on the dance floor like two little poodles," Becca moaned.

I sat up. "Thanks for the image, Becs.

I'll carry that around with me the rest of the day."

"Don't worry, Val, we'll warn you if they get too close," Kelly told me. She swigged from her Nalgene again and screwed the top on, resting it in the grass next to her.

Becca finished her apple and crumpled up the sandwich bag. I leaned back on my hands and gazed at the blue sky. A few puffy clouds skated overhead. The little knots of juniors and seniors scattered over the lawn were breaking up as people headed inside to finish homework or out to their cars to smoke. Next to me, Becca took out her compact and combed her shiny black hair, which already looked perfect. The air was very still and quiet. I closed my eyes and breathed in the smell of clover, listening to the sleepy drone of a bee somewhere nearby.

"Hey!" Kelly said suddenly. We all jumped a little and looked at her. "We still have fifteen minutes. Let's go check out rugby practice."

I shrugged. "Okay."

Becca snapped her compact shut. "Sure. I could use a little eye candy right about now."

We strolled across the lawn toward

the metal bleachers glinting in the sun. A group of seniors was hurtling around the grass like colorful, sweaty gibbons. As we neared the bleachers, Kelly started waving so hard at one big, dark-haired guy that I thought her arm was going to fly off.

"Bruce! Bruce!" she trilled. "Hi!"

"Who's that?" Becca asked. She perched on a bleacher and I slid in beside her.

"Oh my God, he's the best rugby player," Kelly said breathlessly as Bruce lumbered up, patting his face with the hem of his T-shirt, revealing chiseled abs covered with a mat of damp hair.

"What's up, ladies?" Bruce said, breathing heavily. "Hey, Kelly. I saw you in the regional semifinals. Nice finish on the butterfly."

"Thanks. Bruce, these are my friends, Becca and Val."

We all nodded. I glanced at my watch. There were only a few more minutes until the bell, and I still had to get my books for the afternoon. I stood up.

"Cool, nice to meet you, Bruce. Girls, I'm going to go inside—" I was cut off when Kelly grabbed my arm and yanked me back down on the bleachers. I sat down on the warm metal hard.

"So you guys should have seen the amazing goal Bruce scored during the scrimmage last week," Kelly twittered. She kept a firm hold on my arm. I glanced at the Bruce under discussion. He flashed a massive grin in my direction.

I smiled back politely and glanced over at Kelly. "You're hurting my wrist," I hissed through clenched teeth.

She let go carefully, as if releasing a potentially rambunctious dog from the leash. When she had apparently assured herself that I was going to remain sitting, she got to her feet, leaving barely six inches of space between me and the hulk of sweating masculinity that was Bruce the Rugby Player. Then she stood in front of us, staring at me.

"What, Kel?" I asked. "Do I have some lunch on my face?"

She started a little. "Oh, no. You don't. Oh my gosh!" She clapped her hand to her mouth. We all looked at her.

"What?" I asked.

"You know, I'm just *so* thirsty," she said. She wiped her brow as if it were dripping, even though it was only about seventy out.

"I've got some water in my bag," Bruce offered. He half rose from the bleacher. "I'll just go get it."

"No!" Kelly shouted and pushed him back down. He blinked and sat with a thump. "Ah, actually, I meant, no thanks, Bruce. I'm craving a Diet Coke, that's all. I'll just go inside and buy one."

"The vending machines are turned off during lunch," Becca pointed out.

"Oh yeah. Um, I'll just get one out of my locker. Come with me, Bec."

Becca snorted. "No." She glared at Kelly, remaining glued to the bleacher. Kelly shifted her weight back and forth for a moment, then turned and rushed toward the school.

"So, Val, you ever try rugby?" Bruce rumbled.

"Er, no. I haven't." I glanced at Becca, whose eyebrows were knit anxiously.

"Well, hey, anytime you want a private lesson, I'd be happy to show you—"

Becca popped up from the bleacher. "Ooh, Bruce," she cooed, plopping herself right down in between us. "Guess what? I just learned to read palms. Here, let me see yours." She grabbed his massive, sweaty hand and turned it over. I gaped at her, moving over a few inches to extract my suddenly squashed thigh. Bruce looked surprised but submitted happily. "This is your love line," she murmured. Bruce was now gazing dreamily at the top of her head.

Suddenly, Kelly reappeared, walking rapidly toward us. Her hands were empty.

"What happened to your Diet Coke?" I asked as she approached.

"I, um, drank it inside," she said, her eyes darting from Bruce to Becca to me and back again. "What are you doing, *Becca*?" she asked pointedly. "Did you learn fortune telling on your last D and G shopping trip?"

Becca narrowed her eyes at Kelly. "For your information, my grandmother taught me. I wouldn't expect you to understand, though. I don't think they teach it in Jock School."

Kelly suddenly shifted gears. "Hey, you left your lights on in the Beemer this morning. I saw it when I was getting my drink."

Becca bolted up from the bleacher. "Shoot! I had to call Triple A last time—my mom's going to kill me if it happens again."

Kelly widened her eyes. "I know, I know! That's why I came back to tell you."

Becca rushed off across the grass, already rummaging in her bag for her keys. The three of us sat silently, staring at the brilliant green of the playing field in front of us. Faint shouts echoed from the rugby players. Bruce was sitting very close to me. The edge of his sweaty jersey brushed my arm. His stertorous breathing was loud in my ear. I glanced up at him. There was the beginning of a zit on the side of his nose. He smiled at me again and edged a little closer.

Kelly slid carefully off the end of the bleacher. "Hey, I'm going to go back and get a head start on my American history reading—you know how I like to work ahead." Her voice was a shade too loud.

I rose to my feet. "Okay, I'll come with you. The first bell's about to ring anyway."

"Yeah, I'd better get going too." Bruce also stood up.

Kelly sat down abruptly. "On second thought, maybe I'll just stay here and do the reading. You guys go ahead and walk back together."

Faintly, from the school building, the

bell chimed. I grabbed Kelly's hand and pulled her up. "Come on. We're going to be late."

As Kelly and I hurried across the grass together, leaving Bruce trudging well behind us, I hissed, "You're so obvious."

She gazed at me innocently. "What do you mean?"

I rolled my eyes and pushed the school doors open, letting us into the stream of students filling the halls. "I know you're just shoving guys at me to get me to break the GNBP. But seriously, you're going to have to do better than Bruce the Sweaty. I'm really not into all that body hair. Think more like that guy Craig from your party."

"Oh." Kelly seemed taken aback. "Okay, thanks for the tip."

"Sure."

"Oh, girls!" We looked up to see Mrs. Masterson in front of us in the hall, her curly red-brown hair disheveled as usual, waving a handful of papers. "Kelly and Val. Just who I was looking for! Come in here for a minute." She gestured to an empty classroom on our right.

We stepped into the relative silence of the room and Mrs. Masterson spread the papers out on a desk in front of us. "I'm tracking down each of the students who still haven't turned in their junior community-service projects. I don't have papers from either of you yet. Now, are you expecting to work on the group food-bank project or will you be taking the individual option?" She poised her pen over the forms expectantly.

"You can put me down for the group option," Kelly told her.

"Val?"

"Um . . ." The thought of carting around boxes of canned goods while fending off the advances of Kevin and Company at the same time was less than appealing. "I'm going to do an individual project, I think."

She made a little tickmark on her list. "That's fine, but the forms are due tomorrow, you might remember."

I swallowed. That was sooner than I had thought. "Okay, no problem," I said with a blitheness I was far from feeling. "I'll have the form to you by tomorrow."

"Excellent." She gathered up her papers and swept from the room, just as the students began to trickle into the classroom.

"Val, how are you going to come up with a project by tomorrow?" Kelly asked as we parted by the science corridor.

"Kel. Remember who you're talking to. *Of course* I'll come up with something." I waved at her as I headed into anatomy, trying to feel as confident as I sounded.

Eight

Becca grabbed me as I was getting my homework stuff out of my locker after last period and hustled me to the car.

"I still need my anatomy text!" I protested.

"Shut up!" she ordered. "Just get in the car. I'm getting you out of here."

"What is this, a bank heist? You're acting like James Bond," I told her, sliding onto the buttery leather of the BMW's front seat. "Where are we going, anyway?"

She looked over her shoulder and threw the car in reverse. "Somewhere far, far away." She signaled and turned onto Glengarry.

"Like Cabo?" I asked hopefully. "Because I could really use a vacation right about now."

"Not Cabo, but almost as good. You need

to get away from that school and . . . everything." She made an indeterminate gesture with one hand. "That guy Bruce was practically sitting in your lap today at lunch! I can't believe Kelly is trying to sabotage you like that!"

"Yeah, well, it's all in the name of competition. Don't worry, though. I'm not cracking." I opened the glove compartment and extracted Becca's ever-present bag of Tootsie Roll Pops. Sticking a grape one in my mouth, I sank down in the seat and watched the neighborhoods flash by. Already the plush subdivisions with names like Polo Pointe had given way to tall brick houses crowded tightly together. Collapsing chain-link fences lined tiny downtrodden yards and rusty sedans slouched at the curb.

"This is a unique choice of after-school hangout, Bec," I said around my Tootsie Pop. "Are you interested in getting your tongue pierced, perhaps?"

Becca just smiled and maneuvered the Beemer past a double-parked Penske truck. A young couple with dreads was manhandling a futon down the ramp. "No, we're not getting pierced. But we *are* going to Old Court."

I inhaled a shred of grape lollipop and launched into a prolonged coughing fit. "I'm sorry," I said when I had recovered. "It's just that I thought you said we were going down to Old Court." Old Court was the hipster section of town near the university, where all the arty and indie-rock kids hung out. We'd never actually been there, but it was supposed to be fairly cool if you were into vinyl and faux-hawks. Which we weren't.

"I told you, you need to get away," Becca said. "I heard there's this coffeehouse that's supposed to be really cool. And I guarantee there won't be anyone we know there either." She smiled with satisfaction and raked a hand through her silky hair.

"You do know that it's *not* Lilly Pulitzer Day down there, right?" I asked, indicating Becca's pink Lacoste shirt and green-striped cloth belt.

"Ha-ha," she said, unfazed. "Look for a meter, will you?"

"Okay. There's one by the S and M shop." I pointed at a storefront displaying a mannequin dressed in a hot-pink leather corset, black fishnets, and a bullwhip. Her head had been removed and was tucked underneath her arm like a football.

Becca glanced over. I saw her take a deep breath. "This is going to be awesome, don't worry," she said.

"Are you trying to convince me, or yourself?" I got out of the car.

"Look, that's it." Becca pointed to a three-story brick house across the street with a large plate-glass window in front. STERNWELL'S was carved into the ornate wooden sign creaking over the door.

We crossed the street. There was some kind of painting project going on against one wall of the building—a section of the brick was painted white and a canvas tarp was littered with open paint cans and long brushes. Steam fogged the front window, the lower half of which was plastered with hand-drawn flyers for upcoming concerts. *The Dopamines, Bikehaus, 9 p.m.,* read one.

When we pushed open the door, the rich, smoky aroma of roasted coffee beans rolled out at us, mixed with memories of ancient cigarettes and the damp sheep smell of wool sweaters. Mismatched tables and chairs were crammed in everywhere, and the dark wood floor was scarred from years of use. Potted ferns crowded the windows. Framed pastel sketches hung haphazardly on the walls. I peered at one near me, which depicted a very fat man lounging on a sofa, wearing nothing but an orange fedora. I looked away fast.

At the table nearest us, a woman with a long braided ponytail was hunched over a stack of papers, marking them furiously with a pen. Two gray-bearded men were playing chess by the window, and clustered around a long table near the back was a group of hipster types wearing mutton-chops and old gas-station-attendant jackets. They were arguing over a bunch of black-and-white posters spread out on the table in front of them.

Becca and I huddled just inside the door. Conversation hadn't exactly come to a screeching halt upon our entrance, but the paper-marking woman raised her head and gave us a long appraising stare. I offered a weak little smile. She gazed at me blankly and then returned to her papers.

"This was a brilliant idea," I whispered to Becca. She shoved me in the small of the back.

"Let's get something," she whispered back.

A high wooden counter stretched across

one end of the room, dominated by a huge ornate brass espresso machine. Thick, chipped mugs and saucers were stacked in tipsy towers nearby and piled high in a sink behind the counter. A brief menu was scrawled on a blackboard propped on the floor.

I trailed in her wake as she strode purposefully toward the battered counter.

"What can I get you guys?" the barista asked.

I almost fell over onto the really dirty floor. It was the guy from the party, Adam. Only now he was wearing a black apron tied around his waist and—I squinted—a white tunic embroidered with frogs down the front. And skinny jeans. They were really tight.

"Hey, Val!" Adam said, smiling. "Great to see you again. I didn't know you guys came here." His icy blue-gray eyes crinkled up at the corners.

"Hi, Adam. This is our first time here." I cast a sidelong glance at Becca. She was standing very still, staring at Adam, her eyes narrowed. I saw her eyes take in the frog tunic and then the skinny jeans. I nudged her in the ribs.

"Bec? Remember Adam from the party?" I prompted her.

She seemed to snap out of whatever trance Adam's unfortunate fashion sense had put her in. "Oh! Yeah, I remember. Hi. I didn't know you worked here." She gave him a surprisingly friendly smile, considering how rude she'd been to him in Kelly's kitchen. "Can I get a cappuccino?"

"Sure thing." Adam turned several handles and the giant espresso machine started thumping and hissing like an ancient radiator. After a minute, he pushed a cup mounded with foam toward Becca. "Here you go."

"Thanks," she said. "That looks so good."

"Can I get a latte?" I asked.

"Sure." He turned back to the insane espresso machine. A whacking sound emanated from the interior and steam began issuing from several crevices.

"Does he always dress like that?" Becca hissed as Adam busied himself with milk and little shot glasses of espresso.

"How should I know?" I whispered back. "This is only the second time I've ever met him. Anyway, he's nice—kind of dorky, but really nice. So shut up."

"One café latte." Adam pushed a cup the

size of a soup bowl across the counter.

"Thanks." I tried to extract a few bills but my wallet slipped from my sweaty hands. I watched in dismay as about twenty dollars in change clattered to the floor and rolled into various dark corners.

"Oh, great!" I bent to gather the coins, taking down a straw dispenser on the counter with me. A gazillion straws joined my change on the floor. "Oh, crap!" I gazed at the mess in dismay. Becca and I crouched down on the floor, trying to corral the straws.

Adam leaned over the counter. "Guys, don't worry about it," he said. "I'll get the broom out."

"Hey there, can I help you?" a melodious voice asked.

I looked up to see a tall college-age girl standing over us. Her long brown hair was pulled into a loose braid over one shoulder. She wore a simple blue cotton shirtdress and leather Naots.

Awkwardly, I rose to my feet. "I'm sorry," I said. "We can pay for them." I reached into my bag.

The girl laughed. "Don't worry about it. There's always too much stuff stacked on that counter anyway. I'm Sarah, by the way, the manager." She grinned mischievously. "We'll get Adam to clean up. Oh, servant boy!" she called behind her.

Adam heaved an exaggerated sigh and extracted a grimy broom and dustpan from a little closet in the corner. "Jeez, you just never get tired of cracking the whip, do you?" he teased. He rolled his eyes in our direction. "Like *she's* ever busy. All she does is sit back in that office and shuffle papers." He swiped a clump of straws into the dustpan.

Sarah snorted. "What I'm actually doing is trying to keep this place from bleeding to death." She ducked behind the counter and drew a hissing jet of water into a mug. She dropped in a tea bag, pulled out a chair at a nearby table, and sank into it as if her feet hurt. "Phewww," she exhaled. "Yeah, if I didn't have Adam to basically run everything, I'd be even more panicked." She smiled at Adam, who was leaning back against the counter, broom in hand.

"I know, I know, you can't live without me," he responded. They both laughed as if this was a running joke between them.

I looked from one to the other. Were

they together? There was a definite flirty vibe going on, but she had to be at least twenty-two. *Anyway, why are you even thinking about that, Val?* I asked myself sternly. *Who cares if he's hooking up with his boss?*

"She's got me slaving away at this mural outside, hours and hours every day, just so the place looks good when the big boss comes to inspect," Adam said to us. "I'm, like, *dying* out there in the heat." He looked over at Sarah, laughing.

She reached over and slapped his arm. "Yeah, yeah, cry me a river."

"Is that the painting stuff we saw outside?" Becca sat down next to Sarah. I perched on the edge of another chair, trying not to stare at Sarah's perfect tan. It looked almost too good to be real, but she didn't really look like the type to go tanning. Too earthy-crunchy for that.

Sarah nodded. "Right. Adam's doing this mural on the side of the building for his senior community-service project. It's also to spruce the place up. The building owner is coming for an inspection in June and I want everything to look really good. He's always threatening to shut us down."

"I'm just a hair behind schedule." Adam

slid behind the counter again and started unloading a small dishwasher. "I've never done a mural before, and it's taking me a little longer than I thought."

"The juniors have to do a community service project too," I said. "But I haven't thought of mine yet." I tentatively took a sip of my foam-laden coffee and spluttered a little. It was boiling hot.

Sarah looked at Adam across the table and raised her eyebrows. He gave a little shrug and nodded. Sarah leaned toward me. "This might seem totally crazy, but would you consider helping Adam with the painting for your project? It would make the work go twice as fast."

I blinked. "Um, well . . . I don't know." I glanced at Becca. She was sitting very still. I saw her gaze travel from Sarah to Adam and back again. She seemed to be considering something. Then suddenly, she straightened up.

"Val, that is an awesome idea." She banged her palm on the table. "You should totally do the mural here for your project!"

I kicked her leg under the table. *What are you doing?* I mouthed furiously when she looked over. She shot me a huge smile, then leaned over the table toward Sarah. "This is just what Val needs—school's been kind of rough for her lately, you know what I mean?"

"Oh yeah? Well, it's really quiet here." Sarah looked over at me.

"Uh . . ." I glanced at Adam. He was leaning back against the counter again, his face inscrutable. Did he even want my help? "Uh . . ." *Doing good, Val.*

"Adam, Val's, like, *amazing* at drawing," Becca said.

"Actually, it's painting," Adam pointed out.

"Right, that's what I meant." Becca didn't miss a beat.

"Um, but . . . ," I sputtered.

Beside me, Becca was still chattering on merrily. "Okay, so what's your cell?" she asked Adam. When I didn't move, she poked me in the ribs. I jumped and pulled out my phone.

He gave me his number. I looked up and he held my gaze for a second. I felt my face grow warm.

"Okay!" Sarah stood up. "It's settled, then. Can you come on Wednesday, Val? That would be awesome."

"Yeah, I guess."

"See you Wednesday," Adam said cheerfully.

"Sure," I mumbled. Leaving our almost-full coffee cups and pulling the smiling, waving Becca behind me, I somehow made my way to the door, trying to tamp down the rising sense that nothing that had happened in the last twenty minutes had been within my control.

Nine

"What was going on in there?" I exploded at Becca once we were safely ensconced in the BMW again. "One minute, I'm ordering coffee, the next I'm doing craft projects in hippie paradise. What got into you? Were you suddenly possessed by the ghost of Janis Joplin?"

Becca smiled beatifically as she steered us back toward home. "You know, that really did work out beautifully. I had no idea."

"What worked out?"

She glanced over at me. "Look, don't you see how perfect this is? You need to get away from all those stupid guys at school if you want to keep the GNBP going, right? I mean, do you really want to work on that group food-bank project?"

"No, I told Mrs. Masterson to put me down for the individual option."

Becca banged her hand on the steering wheel. "So? You can escape to Sternwell's. Really, you should be thanking me."

"Oh yeah? How come working with this guy every day, just the two of us, wouldn't violate the GNBP?"

She waved her hand in the air. "You said yourself that you're allowed to *talk* to guys. Besides, one, he's totally with that girl Sarah. And two, when did you start going for guys with frogs on their shirts?"

"You really think he's with that girl?"

Becca cast me a sideways glance. "Duh. They might as well have had a poster: 'Sexual Tension Here.' Anyway, who cares? That just makes it better for you."

"Yeah, I know." She was right, of course. So much better for the GNBP if Adam was attached already.

"Right. So there, it's settled." She smiled.

"Wow, you're hard-core about this bet, aren't you? I don't know, I think you'd look kind of cute in the purple dress," I teased.

"Very funny. It would go with Kelly's blond hair *so* much better." She slowed for a red light. "Guess what I heard today?"

"What?" I rummaged through my bag, looking for a piece of gum.

"Mr. Solis is making the entire junior and senior classes take a ballroom-dancing lesson in the gym in two weeks!" Mr. Solis was our hideously enthusiastic new vice principal—the kind of guy you really wish would get a life so he'd leave yours alone.

"Are you kidding?" I scraped some lint from the lone piece of Eclipse I'd unearthed at the bottom of my bag. "Are we all auditioning for *Dancing With the Stars?*"

Becca shook her head. "It's to get ready for prom. He says he doesn't want us looking like a bunch of hooligans on the dance floor." She guffawed.

"Wait, he actually said 'hooligans'?"

"I know. He's hopeless." Her brow was furrowed. "So how're you going to swing this one? It'll violate the GNBP to actually dance with a guy, right?"

"Um, yeah, I guess it would." I clicked my tongue, thinking. "Okay, I've got it. Simple. I just won't go." I popped the gum in my mouth and winced as I bit down. Definitely very old gum.

"Oh yeah, I forgot to mention that attendance *with* a partner is mandatory." Becca glanced over at me, her face anxious. "You'll think of something, won't you, Val?"

"Watch it! You almost hit that garbage can." Damn. Damn, damn, damn. I cleared my throat. "Of course I'll think of something. And it'll be a brilliant solution. Did you forget who you're talking to?" I grabbed my bag as Becca pulled up in front of my house and mustered the strength to wave cheerfully until the Beemer had disappeared down the block. Only then did I let my hand wilt and my shoulders slump. This was just great. Now, on top of the whole mural situation, I had to figure out a way to go to this stupid lesson with a partner who wasn't a date. *And* the Saab was in the driveway, which meant Mom was home.

"Hi," I called softly as I opened the front door. Maybe she'd be busy in the studio and I could just slip upstairs. It wasn't Mom in particular, I just didn't want to talk to *anyone* right now.

"Hi, honey!" Mom called from the kitchen. "Come in here and tell me about your day."

I let my shoulders sag, and my book bag fell heavily to the floor with a thump. I slowly headed for the kitchen. Mom was whisking around between the counters and the stove, throwing carrots and potatoes into a pot of boiling water. She wiped her forehead on a dish towel as I came in and sat down at the table with a sigh of relief. "Oof. My feet."

I opened the refrigerator door and examined the contents.

"Don't eat!" Mom ordered. "Dinner in twenty minutes."

"Mom, I'm starving." Withered green peppers, banana bread, plain yogurt, leftover spaghetti. I took out a tub of hummus and rummaged in the cabinet for pita chips. "Just a little."

Mom patted the seat of the chair across from her. "So, how was school?"

I shrugged, leaning back against the counter, and scraped up some hummus with a chip. "Okay. It was kind of a rough day."

"How come?" Mom looked concerned. "Is it that American history test?"

I sighed. It would be nice to confess everything that had been happening, but really, I didn't want Mom to have a stroke or something. My problems were so, so much more complicated than an American history test. "No, it's not that." Seeing her mouth open to follow up with another question, I hurried on. "Hey, Becca took me to this coffeehouse after school, Sternwell's?"

She nodded. "Is that area safe for you alone?"

I tried not to roll my eyes and almost succeeded. "I was with Becca, okay?" I stuffed another chip into my mouth. "Anyway, Becca and I started talking to this girl Sarah, the manager, and then the next thing I know, I'm signed up for my community service project there, with this guy I don't even know!" I poked my hand in the bag for another chip, but Mom rose crisply and whisked it away.

"So you finally have a project! Isn't the deadline tomorrow?" She capped the hummus and stuck it back in the fridge, then peered at the boiling carrots. She unwrapped a tray of cubed beef and slid the meat into the water. "I'm so glad you finally chose something."

"But I didn't really *choose* it," I protested. "I just got roped into it. And I don't even know this guy!"

"What is the project, anyway?" Mom asked, stirring the pot with a big wooden spoon.

"Painting a mural!" I flung my hands out at my sides. "See? There's no way I can do it—I don't know anything about painting."

Mom put the spoon down and turned to face me. "Val, you need a project. Here is one." She put her hands on her hips. "Go get the form."

"But, Mom—"

"Go get it." She turned back to the stew.

I dragged myself to the hall and returned with the form, which had been folded up in my calc binder for the last two months. I spread it in front of me on the kitchen table. "I don't have a pen," I tried.

Without pausing from her stirring, Mom stuck her hand in the junk drawer and tossed over a green Magic Marker.

I was distinctly nervous as I filled out the different blanks describing the type of project, duration, location. I mean, aside from the party and seeing him that afternoon, I barely knew Adam. Who says he even wanted me there, anyway?

Even so, after dinner that night, I retreated to my room and shut the door behind me, muffling the sound of Mom and

Dad laughing over their glasses of wine in the kitchen. I flopped onto my bed, yanking my anatomy workbook and facedown copy of *Hamlet* out from under me, and pulled out my phone.

It wasn't like I had a whole lot of other options. *Hey. Everything's set,* I typed. *See you on Wednesday.* I stared out the window next to my bed. This could actually work out fine. I could get away from the stalkers at school, the work would be easy, and nice, friendly Adam wouldn't distract me from the main goal: the successful completion of the GNBP.

Ten

At school that week, Willy seemed sufficiently depressed by the cookie incident to stay away. But Kevin had developed the disconcerting habit of leering at me in the hallway every morning when I passed him on the way to anatomy. I started going outside the building and coming in the gym doors just so I wouldn't have to see him. After a long conversation with Brian North outside the lunchroom one day, in which I explained no less than six times that I *could not* go to his youth group dance, Sternwell's was seeming more and more like an oasis shimmering on the horizon.

When Wednesday afternoon arrived, I put on an army green T-shirt, my oldest jeans, and a pair of flip-flops and gingerly drove the Saab over to Old Court. The neighborhood seemed seedier than I remembered—broken glass glinting on the sidewalk, honeysuckle and scrubby mulberry trees pushing through the crumbling asphalt in the vacant lots. Tall, narrow brick buildings crowded close to the sidewalk, six or eight long windows in front. Peeling advertisements for cell phones or pizza delivery services were painted on the windowless sides. A brown bottle with a faded Colt 45 label rolled away from my feet as I got out of the car, and a beetle scuttled out of the mouth.

Around the corner of the building, Adam was perched on an eight-foot wooden ladder, methodically spreading sky blue paint back and forth with a wide brush. Off to one side, a canvas tarp was spread with a huge assortment of paint cans, brushes of different sizes, scrapers, rollers, and a big sheet of paper. The whole side of the building had been scrubbed and freshly painted white, the bright paint made even brighter by the old, soft red brick surrounding it.

"Hi," I said, dropping my bag at my

feet. Adam glanced over his shoulder and flashed a brief smile.

"Hi," he replied, and then turned back around. The frog tunic was mercifully gone today, replaced by a paint-splattered white T-shirt. The silence stretched on. Adam continued painting, while I continued feeling extra-specially awkward. Finally, I hitched my bag back over my shoulder. This was stupid. He obviously didn't want me here, just like I thought. I turned to go, just as Adam set his brush down on the top of the ladder and climbed down.

"Sorry about that," he said, wiping his hands on his jeans. "This stuff dries incredibly fast, so I had to finish that section." He bent down to a big tray of the blue paint and stirred it with a flat stick. The edge of his T-shirt pulled up a little, showing a smooth, tanned band of skin above the waist of his jeans.

He straightened up and pointed to a battered roller leaning against the wall. "You can start filling in that first piece over there." He indicated a large section of the wall marked with tape. "It's the dark red paint in that tray." Without waiting for a reply, he climbed to the top of his ladder and resumed painting.

Well, okay. That was a little abrupt. I mean, I didn't need hugs and flowers, but a little "please" never hurt anybody. But whatever. I could handle it. I dropped my bag on the ground again and grabbed the roller.

Back and forth. I watched the deep red slowly consuming the gleaming white base coat. The roller made a soft zipping sound as I pushed it methodically. *Ziiip. Ziiip.* The shouts of some kids playing basketball in the lot across the street floated over to us. The only other sound was the creaking of the rickety wooden ladder under Adam's weight. *Ziiip.* It was kind of hypnotic in a way. *Ziiip.* Then, from the front of the building, I heard the squeak of a door and then the crunch of footsteps on the gravel. I looked up. Sarah was coming toward us. She was wearing a white apron tied over jeans and her hair was twisted in two braids that bounced on her shoulders when she walked.

"Hi, guys." She stopped at the base of Adam's ladder. "How's it going, Val?"

"Hi. Good. I just got here." I gestured to my roller. "Adam's put me to work already."

"Finally, someone to order around!" Adam called down at us. "Such a relief."

Sarah laughed. "I know, you've been waiting for this day for so long, haven't you?" She looked at me. "Have a good time, Val. Don't let this guy get too bossy, okay?" She waved at us as she disappeared around the corner of the building again.

Silence descended. Adam's eyes were fixed on the wall as he carefully outlined his section in thin blue lines. A mourning dove cooed at us from a nearby mulberry branch. I could hear my stomach digesting the bagel and cream cheese I'd eaten after school. Finally, I couldn't stand it anymore. "So how did you get started working here?" I asked. My voice rang in the quiet. I winced. Luckily, Adam didn't seem to notice.

"Sarah's a friend of my older sister," he said. "She was always around our house when we were growing up. So she was looking for someone to work the counter last year, and I need some extra cash." He shrugged and dipped his brush into the small can of blue balanced on the top of the ladder. "It worked out really well."

"Oh, you've known her for a long time?"

It wasn't my business, really, but the words came out before I could stop them.

Adam finished the blue lines and climbed down from the ladder. "I guess." He picked up a handful of dirty brushes that were lying on the tarp and dunked them in a waiting bucket of water, swishing them back and forth.

"So she's in college?" *Val, stop. You're sounding obsessive.* I couldn't help it. Anyway, I was just asking friendly questions.

"She's part-time, but her fiancé's graduating soon, so she's going to start going full-time." He dumped the bucket of now cloudy blue water onto the grass and laid the clean brushes out in a neat row to dry in the sun.

I leaned my roller against the wall and took a deep breath. "She's getting married?" I bent and brushed some gravel dust off the tops of my feet so I wouldn't have to look at him.

Adam looked up, his brows knit a little. "Yeah. I'm actually going to be in her wedding in July. You sound surprised."

"Oh! Um, well, to be totally honest, I thought that . . ." I could feel my cheeks growing hot.

"That what?" Adam looked puzzled.

"Wait, you thought that she and I . . . ?" He started laughing.

My face felt like it was going to burst into flame. "Well, yeah." I seized the roller again and began zipping it back and forth vigorously. Little droplets of red paint flew from the end.

"Hey, watch it there," Adam said. He grabbed a wet rag out of another water bucket and wiped at the red splatters. "Wow, that's hilarious. No, Sarah's like another sister." He dropped the rag into the bucket. "And dating family members really isn't my thing."

I forced a short laugh, trying to readjust my brain at the same time. Good thing Becca wasn't here for this conversation. She'd never have pushed me to work with Adam if she'd known he wasn't attached.

"So how about you?" Adam asked. "Are you seeing anyone?"

I glanced at him sharply but he was drying his hands on an old towel. His voice sounded completely casual.

"Not really," I said. I wasn't quite ready to tell him about Dave—and the GNBP was most definitely off-limits. "Hey, you know . . ." I cast around for something to distract him.

"It's—it's kind of hard painting this thing without knowing what it's going to look like. What is it, like a ship or something?"

Adam laughed. "Not exactly." He motioned me over to a big piece of paper unrolled in a corner. A few rocks weighed down the edges. "This is a sketch of what we'll be painting," he said, pointing with his pencil. I peered over his shoulder and my eyes widened.

In the center of the paper spread a gorgeous explosion of yellow, orange, and red petals, opening on the page like a chrysanthemum on acid. At first glance, it did look like a flower, but when I studied it more closely, I saw that the petals also looked like flames. At the center of the flame-flower, blue and black feathers waved as if trapped.

"Wow, did you draw that?" I asked.

"Yeah," Adam said, staring down at the drawing. His cheeks were pink.

"It's really good," I told him. "It's going to look incredible on the wall."

He blinked. "Thanks," he said slowly. A little grin hovered around his mouth. "I'm glad you appreciate it." The grin widened.

I poked his arm. "Are you surprised or something? I'm not a *total* ditz, despite what you might think. I actually do like good art."

Adam leaned back on his hands and grinned at me. "No, I'm not surprised. I could tell the minute I met you that you were a girl with excellent taste. After all, you liked the drawing I did of you, right?"

"Of course."

"See? Excellent taste." He studied me for a moment, then got up, dusting the grass off the rear of his jeans. "Be right back. I just have to grab something inside."

"Okay," I said. I sat back on the grass and drew my knees up. I heard his footsteps crunching away and the distant creak of the coffeehouse door. Then silence. The sun was baking the top of my head. The basketball-playing kids had evidently gone inside and the mourning dove was taking a break. I stared idly across the street at a row of battered parked cars, the sun glinting off their windshields. Just then, my phone buzzed. I glanced at the screen. Kelly. I flipped the phone open.

"Hi," I said. "What's up?"

"Hi!" Kelly and Becca chirped at the same time. "It's us."

"Why are you guys calling?" I said.

"Just wanted to see how the painting's

going," Kelly bubbled. "It's kind of warm out. Has he taken his shirt off yet?"

"*No*, he has not taken his shirt off." I glanced at the coffeehouse door.

"Just ignore her, Val!" Becca said in the background. "Just focus on painting, okay?"

"Well, that's what I'm *trying* to do," I told them.

"Where is he now?" Kelly asked.

"He's inside getting something, okay, nosy? Butt out, will you, guys? I don't need you to check up on me."

"Diamonds, Val, diamonds!" Becca reminded me.

I could hear the sound of someone grabbing at the phone. "Purple dress, Val!" Kelly shouted.

The coffeehouse door creaked again. Adam crunched up next to me. "I made us some drinks," he said, slightly out of breath.

"Guys, I have to go," I hissed and hung up on them. I looked up. He was holding two coffees in big ceramic mugs. A mound of fluffy whipped cream crowned each of them, and caramel drizzled down the sides. Dark chocolate shavings were sprinkled on top, and a wafer was perched on the side.

I blinked. My mouth started watering. "Wow. Thanks."

He managed to sit down without spilling any of the coffee and offered me one of the mugs. I stretched out my hand to accept and then stopped. His whole face had a pink sheen and his gaze hovered somewhere near the ground between us. A little alarm bell started clanging inside my head. Unattached guy. Sweet little gift. Shy smile. *GNBP! GNBP!* an imaginary loudspeaker blared. Adam looked up, right into my eyes. That was it.

I took a deep breath. "Um, listen, Adam."

"Yeah?"

"Um, this is kind of awkward to say." I looked down at the ground and picked up a little pebble.

"Uh-oh." He set the coffees down on the ground. "This doesn't sound good."

I nodded. "Well, it's not bad or anything. It's just that, you know, I'm really not looking to go out with anyone right now. Like at all." I made myself look right at him, which was hard when his face was so crestfallen.

"Oh. That's cool." He picked up a stick and started tracing a pattern in the dirt, not meeting my eyes. The coffees sat like homeless little orphans at his side.

"It's not you," I said. "I'm just taking a break, that's all. I think we should just be friends, okay?"

"Yeah, of course." He got to his feet, still not looking at me, and dusted off the rear of his jeans. He picked up the coffees and handed me one. "Well, anyway, this one's yours."

I stood up also, balancing the coffee. It smelled great, but was accepting it a GNBP violation now that we had agreed to be friends? Gray area, I decided. Better to err on the side of caution. I shoved the mug back at him, a little harder than I intended. The whipped cream slopped over the side and a wave of coffee baptized the front of his T-shirt. "Actually, no thanks," I said. "I just remembered that I'm, um, allergic to coffee. It makes me break out in hives." I continued holding out the cup.

Adam looked confused. "But didn't you have a latte when you came in that first time?" he asked.

I cringed. "Er, yeah, I did . . ." My voice trailed off. Then I had a flash of brilliance. "Actually that was when I realized I was allergic."

Adam raised his eyebrows.

"Yeah, I went home that night and was

completely covered in hives. I couldn't even see my eyes," I said, trying to sound convincing. "They were, like, all puffed up. It was gross."

"Oh," he said. "But wouldn't—"

This was getting difficult. Better retreat. As casually as I could, I plucked my bag from the ground and hoisted it over my shoulder. "You know, I just remembered I have to do some chores for my mom."

"Oh, okay . . ." Adam still held the sloppy coffee cup cradled in his hands while the other, perfect coffee steamed on the grass next to him.

"See you later." I forced myself to walk slowly to my car, knowing he was watching me the whole way. I exhaled only when I had slid behind the baking hot steering wheel. I threw the car into drive and craned over my shoulder to maneuver it out of the narrow parking space. *Good work, Val. Potentially disastrous GNBP-wrecking situation nicely diffused.* No feelings were hurt, boundaries were firmly established. I shook off the memory of Adam's downcast face. The GNBP's future had never looked brighter.

Eleven

I'd been hoping for a massive thunderstorm to give me an excuse to stay away from the coffeehouse and any more potential conflict with the GNBP, but the next day was sunny and hot, as if summer had decided to arrive two months early. What was I afraid of, anyway? I asked myself, as I drove over to Sternwell's. A random arty guy who occasionally wears skinny jeans? Definitely not. I'd dealt with way more difficult situations than this. It was simple: no more little chatty sessions with coffee on the grass. Just paint the mural and get the project over with as fast as possible.

The little pep talk helped immensely and I stepped from the Saab with renewed confidence. Today, I was going to project just the right air—polite, distant, and cool. Like an ice queen. I kept the image of the purple dress firmly fixed in my mind as a detriment. I rounded the corner and saw Adam up on his ladder. A steaming cup of chai sat on the ground next to him.

"Hey," I said.

Adam turned around. "Hey. Glad you came back. I thought you might be at home, you know, with your eyes all squished up."

I couldn't help laughing a little. "Yeah, well, luckily for you I'm not. But I can't drink that, okay?" I indicated the chai and stared him right in the eyes so he couldn't miss my meaning.

The corners of Adam's mouth twitched. He climbed down from the ladder and picked up the cup. "That's too bad," he said slowly, bringing it to his nose and inhaling the fragrant aroma. "But it would be even worse if it was for you in the first place." He tilted the cup to his lips and took a sip, watching me over the top.

"Oh!" I blinked. "Er, that's cool. I just thought—," I stuttered. Then I looked up. He was still watching me, his face bland, but I caught the crinkles around his eyes. "Wait a minute . . ."

He laughed and thrust the warm, heavy cup into my hands. "Of course it's for you. I really don't want you to swell up like a bullfrog, but I figured you could handle a chai. I promise you won't regret it."

The steam rising from the milky tea was scented with cardamom and ginger. "Mmm," I murmured involuntarily. I took a little sip. Sweet, creamy, and spicy. I couldn't help smiling and Adam smiled back, a basic friendly smile. Maybe I was being too strict. I mean, a chai could be just a chai. "Thanks." I took another sip.

He picked up a large tube of dandelion yellow and squirted some into a bucket. "No problem. It's the least I can do since you're helping me." He trickled in a thin stream of white, stirring with a flat stick.

There. He said it himself. It was like a trade. Chai for painting. No GNBP violation at all. I relaxed and picked up my friend the roller, which was sitting head down in a water tub. "What am I doing, more of this red?"

Adam glanced up from his bucket. He was squeezing in orange from a tiny bottle drop by drop. "Yeah, that would be great. Hey, check out this shade." He tilted the bucket in my direction. "You think this would be good for the outer petals?"

I craned my neck. The paint inside was now a creamy yellow. "Isn't it kind of lighter than in the drawing?" I pointed to the large sheet of paper spread on the ground, its corners weighed down with rocks.

He stared at the paint and nodded slowly. "Yeah, I think you're right. But what if I just . . ." He dribbled in a minute bit of red and two drops of purple and stirred again. Now the paint was the vibrant, bold yellow of buttercups.

"Perfect," I told him. I pried the top off a can of red and stirred it with a flat wooden stick. Then I carefully tipped some into a tray. Adam climbed up on his ladder, carrying the bucket with him, and began dotting yellow over yesterday's blue.

I dipped my roller in the paint. "I like the dots," I said, *ziiip*ping the roller up and down the brick again.

"Hey, thanks," he said. "I wasn't sure it was a good idea, but yeah, I like it now too." He leaned back on his ladder to admire his work. I continued rolling. *Ziiip. Ziiip.*

The basketball kids weren't around today, but the mourning dove was back, calling thoughtfully from his branch every now and then. A long, low Cadillac with tinted windows passed by, bass vibrating the undercarriage. I reached the end of the wall and started rolling my way back. I glanced up at Adam. He was still intent on his dots, his face about three inches from the wall.

"So what's the story with you?" I asked. "Are you going to college in the fall, or what?"

Adam blinked and looked down at me almost as if he'd forgotten I was there. "What?"

I raised my voice. *"Are you going to college in the fall?* You're a senior, right?"

He cleared his throat. "Yeah, I am." He coughed a little. "I'm not exactly going to college, though."

I looked up at him. He was back to the dots, but this time, it seemed like more of a way to avoid my eyes.

"Aren't you graduating?"

He nodded, still dotting. "I am. It's just that . . . I don't know, I didn't feel like I'd learn what I wanted at college. So I'm apprenticing with a sculptor in Maine instead."

"Really?" I paused my rolling momentarily. "Are your parents cool with that?"

He shrugged. "Now they are. It took a while for them to get used to the idea. And this guy's studio is, like, way out in the woods. They're kind of worried I'm going to get eaten by a bear or something." He glanced down at me. "I got into college, you know. I was accepted at North City Art Academy. I don't want you to think I'm some kind of slacker or something."

I shook my head. "I don't. Why would I think that? Just because you're not going to college?"

"Well, that's how most people act when I tell them."

"They're just stupid, then. It's not like you're saying you're going to hang out at the beach your whole life or something," I told him. "I'd never have the nerve to just go off and do something like that. It's going to be just the usual for me—graduation, college, job—even if I *wanted* to do something else."

He smiled down at me. "Maybe you should try it sometime." Then, from his high perch, he looked over toward the street. "Hey, isn't that your friend who was in here before?" He pointed with his brush.

"What?" I followed his arm. Becca and Kelly were emerging from a familiar red car pulled up at the curb, pushing their sunglasses up on their heads and looking around. I felt a little surge of irritation. What were they doing, checking up on me? I saw Kelly point to the wooden sign out front and say something to Becca, who nodded. They hadn't seen us around the corner yet. As I watched, they went up the steps and disappeared through the front door.

"I don't even know what they're doing here," I told Adam.

"Maybe they wanted some coffee," he suggested mildly.

I bit my cheek. The last thing I wanted was Adam to get suspicious about my motives for hanging out with him. "Yeah, of course," I agreed.

I wasn't surprised to hear the crunch of shoes on gravel a few minutes later. "Hi, Val!" I heard Becca call out. I turned around casually. She and Kelly were standing a few feet away, both holding steaming cups, their eyes darting around the scene rapidly, taking in the half-painted wall, the brushes, paint cans, buckets, and tarps spread out all over the scrubby grass. "Kelly just had such a craving for a hazelnut latte, so I brought her over," she said brightly. "We saw your, ah, *boss* inside. Sarah, right? She's really pretty. And we wanted to say hi to you too, of course."

I rolled my eyes. "Of course. Hi."

Adam climbed down from the ladder. His hair was splattered lightly with white paint. "Hey. I'm Adam." He stuck out his hand to Kelly and smiled. "Did you guys come to help paint?"

"No, they were just getting coffee and then they're leaving," I broke in, staring pointedly at their innocent faces. "Right, guys?"

"Of course, Val," Becca soothed. She looked over at Adam. "She's so high-strung, isn't she? It's great she's doing this project with you—it's just the break she needs."

Adam nodded agreeably. "Sure, it's great."

"Hello?" I waved my arms. "I'm standing right here. I can actually hear everything you're saying."

"Okay, okay, we're going," Kelly said. She took a last appraising glance around, then shot me a smirky smile. "Don't work too hard, Val." She grinned. "Don't forget to have some fun too." She mouthed *purple dress* at me.

I shook my head slightly and pointed at my ears, then gave her a closed-mouth little smile. "Bye. See you guys later."

"Later!" they trilled and crunched away. A minute later, the Beemer engine fired up and roared away.

I furiously rolled paint onto the wall for a moment. Didn't I have enough going on without those two creeping around and spying on me? I rolled my way to the end of the wall and, with my irritation as momentum, followed the roller right off the corner. I stumbled and caught my balance, just avoiding being impaled by the handle. "Whoops!"

"Are you okay?" Adam looked over.

"Yeah." I set the roller down in a paint tray. "I'm going to take a break for a minute."

Adam laid down his brush. "Me too. Are you hungry?"

"N—," I started to say before I realized that my stomach was rumbling. "What are you, a closet psychic? I'm starving."

"Cool. I know a great place for sand-wiches." He guided me around the corner of the building. "Here's my car," he said.

I looked around. The street was empty except for a fire hydrant and a junked sedan at the curb a few buildings down. "Where?" I asked.

"There." He pointed to the sedan.

"*That's* your car?" I walked over. It was a gray Volvo—or had been at one time. The entire bottom half was covered in rust. Both bumpers were gone, and the roof consisted of a piece of heavy plastic tied down with rope. I peered in the window with difficulty, since it was covered in a layer of sticky dust. Most of the upholstery was gone from the seats, so the foam innards boiled up like mad popcorn. I straightened up. "So what do we do—carry it to the sandwich place on our shoulders?"

Adam grinned. "Yeah, it's a little beat-up. It was my brother's and he kept saying he was going to fix it up, but then he went to college. Now *I* keep saying I'm going to fix it up."

I laughed and wrestled for a minute with the passenger door. Finally it opened with a protesting squeal and I climbed in, fitting my feet in among the pop cans, paintbrushes, newspapers, and CD cases that covered the floor.

Adam turned the ignition and pulled away from the curb. A screech rose from the engine, immediately followed by a scraping so deafening I had to consciously restrain myself from covering my ears. I pressed myself against the seat. Adam must have noticed the grimace on my face because he grinned apologetically and said something incomprehensible.

"What?" I almost yelled.

We bumped over a manhole cover and the scraping mercifully stopped. I shook my head to clear the ringing in my ears.

"Sorry about that," Adam said, now that I could actually hear him. "My tailpipe's broken. It drags on the pavement from time to time. I have to get it fixed."

"Or you could just go deaf," I suggested.

"That's also a possibility. I'm just weighing my options right now." He pulled up in front of a little store with WEAVER ST. CO-OP painted in yellow lettering on the front window, surrounded by swirls and starbursts in blue, green, and red. A bell tinkled overhead as we pushed through the door.

Bins of bulk beans and grains lined the walls, and the few aisles were stacked with bags of dried fruit, nuts, organic pancake mix, and cartons of soy milk. Adam led the way to a few small tables at the back. "The veggie Reuben is amazing," he told me.

"Oh yeah, I'm not surprised," I said, looking at him sideways.

"About what?" He pulled out a wobbly cane-back chair for me.

"Nothing," I said airily. "It's just that I have you pegged. Vegetarian, right?"

He rolled his eyes. "Thanks. I love it when people make random assumptions about me. For your information, I *was* a vegetarian for a couple of years. But I cheated with a bacon cheeseburger. It was all over after that." He shot this last over his shoulder as he spoke to a shaggy-haired guy behind a little counter, returning a few minutes later with toasted rye bread stacked high with grilled, sliced tofu, sauerkraut, and swiss cheese.

"You know, I wasn't just making a random assumption," I said as he set a plate down in front of me. "A lot of, um, art students are vegetarians."

Adam sat down across from me and took a huge bite of his sandwich. "You mean crunchy-granola types, right?" His cheeks were distended as he chewed. He swallowed with difficulty.

"Well . . ." I took a bite of my own sandwich to save myself from answering, losing half the sauerkraut in the process.

"You may not be aware of this, but people are not always what they seem," Adam said, watching me scrape up sauerkraut with my fingers.

I snorted. "Yeah. I learned that particular lesson earlier this year." I mopped up the Thousand Island dressing dripping down my chin.

Adam handed me a stack of napkins. "Would you like a bib? They keep them reserved for only the messiest eaters."

"Hey, I'm trying my best here." Some tofu fell onto my plate. "This sandwich is giving me a hard time."

He nodded. "They've been known to do that." He stuffed the rest of his own sandwich into his mouth. "So what did you mean, you learned that lesson earlier this year?"

I hesitated, then shrugged. If he was apparently the last person in school who didn't know about Dave and me, why deny him a little laugh at my expense? "Do you know Dave Strauss?" I asked.

He shook his head.

"Junior? Tall, brown hair? Basketball forward?"

His face remained blank. "I've never heard of this guy. Did you guys go out or something?"

I resisted the temptation to ask if he'd been living on the moon for the last month. But perhaps assuming that everyone in school knew about my guy problems was just a tad conceited. I looked down at my plate, where a mangled crust of rye bread was sitting alone. "Something like that. It didn't work out, though. Apparently he prefers Strawberry Princess pageant contestants."

Adam nodded. "Yeah, me too."

I looked up. "Really?" My voice rose to a squeak.

"No! Are you serious?" He laughed. "What the heck is a Strawberry Princess?"

I slumped back in my seat. "Sorry. I'm just a little . . . on edge these days."

"Want a root beer?"

"Sure." I stared after him as he retrieved two bottles from a cooler against the wall, trying to figure out why Adam's Strawberry Princess comment would upset me for even a minute. The point of the GNBP was to get *away* from guys, so why should I care?

Before I could muse further, Adam returned. "We should have a toast," he said, sliding one of the drinks over to me. "To Val, who's helping me out of my hole, so Sarah will permit me to go on living." He raised his bottle in my direction. I grinned back and our eyes connected. A little tingle ran through me. We both looked away hurriedly.

I stared at a poster on the wall advertising a long-past Art Garfunkel concert. Adam hummed a little tune. *"Mr. Sandman,"* I thought, still staring at Art. I slid my eyes across, just as Adam was also sneaking a glance at me. I flicked my eyes back to Art. Silence descended.

"So!" Adam said after a long moment. "That dance lesson next week is going to be so hilarious, huh?"

I snorted. "Yeah, it's going to be awesome—learning *salsa*. Has Mr. Solis gone insane? I can't believe it's mandatory either, can you?"

"Like we're not in school enough hours of the day." Adam tilted back in his chair. "Do you have a partner yet?"

"N—," I automatically began to answer. Then I looked at him sharply. Something in his voice made me look up sharply. He was nonchalantly tapping on the edge of the table. "Um . . ."

"I was thinking we could go together." He must have seen the look on my face. "Oh, I mean, just as friends," he quickly said.

"Right . . ." I hesitated. "Look, I don't think I can—"

Adam brought his chair down with a thump and abruptly stood up. "No big deal." He swept all our lunch trash onto a plate in one swift, efficient movement and brought it over to the counter. "Thanks, Rob," he said to the counter guy, who acknowledged him with a wave and a nod. He came back to the table. "Ready?" he said briefly, looking at a point somewhere over my shoulder.

"Yeah," I said slowly, getting up from the table. "Look, Adam . . ."

"I have to get back," he said over his shoulder, already walking toward the door.

I followed, feeling like I had swallowed a chunk of asphalt instead of a veggie Reuben. The tailpipe went into action as we drove down the street, covering our silence. As Adam pulled up to the coffeehouse, I placed my hand on the door handle, and then turned to him. "Adam," I said, not knowing what was going to come next. "About the dance lesson . . ."

This time he waved his hand airily. "It's no big deal." He offered me his relaxed grin. "I'll see you there, okay?"

"Okay," I said after a pause. I shoved hard on the door and it opened with a clank and a scrape. "See you there."

Twelve

Beeep! I laid on the horn of the Saab and waited. The door to Aunt Beth's house remained stubbornly closed. I glanced at the dashboard clock. The dance lesson was supposed to start at seven and we still had to drive there. I blasted the horn again and waited for my dance partner—also known as my thirteen-year-old cousin Larry, also know as my brilliant solution. There was no way taking Larry could violate the rules of the GNBP. He was eighty pounds soaking wet, a foot shorter than me—and *my relative*. I thought of the earrings swinging from my ears on prom night. Or maybe I should let Becca have them and take the necklace. I'd need a dress with a low front for that, though . . .

The front door opened. Larry trudged down the steps, staring at the ground the entire way. Aunt Beth appeared in the doorway behind him, holding a glass of wine.

"Knock 'em dead, you two!" she called, waving. I waved back as Larry slumped in the passenger seat next to me. He folded his arms across his chest and stared darkly out the window as I pulled away from the curb.

I glanced across at him. His straight black hair swung against his cheeks, concealing his eyes. He heaved a deep sigh and slid further down in the seat, propping a giant pair of grubby white sneakers on the dashboard. "Listen, Larry, thanks for being my dance partner," I said. "It's going to be really fast, I promise, okay?" *Darn right it is. Just get to the gym, prance around the room a few times, and get out.*

Larry mumbled something.

"What?" I asked. "I can't hear you."

He raised his voice. "I *said* Assassin's Creed II just came out and I'm going to a stupid dance lesson!"

I saw a break in the boulevard traffic and swung into the left lane. "Well, it's just a game, right? Can't you play it when you get back?"

He shot me a look of utter bitterness. "You know I'm only doing this because Mom said I couldn't go to Extreme Paintball this weekend if I didn't."

When we reached the school, we found the gym packed with the entire junior and senior classes, everyone standing around the perimeter of the gym, talking or sitting on the bleachers. Their voices echoed off the high cinder-block walls. Already the air was steamy with accumulated bodies, and most people were shedding layers.

Up on a riser at one end, a trim dark-haired man in pleated gray slacks was bending over, fiddling with a laptop. An enormous pair of speakers was set up on the floor. Mr. Solis stood at the man's side, hands clasped over his paunch, his sweaty, red face beaming. Off to one side, a folding table held a dozen or so two-liter bottles of soda and several economy-size bags of chips.

With Larry slouching behind me, his hands in his pockets, I snared a cup of Diet Coke from the refreshment table, and then slipped behind the basketball post at one end, hoping to remain as inconspicuous as possible. I scanned the space. Kevin, Travis, and a few other guys were on the bleachers, punching one another. Becca and Kelly were standing with Logan and Brent on the sidelines. Becca was wearing black leggings and a blousy green jersey top, and Kelly was in a baggy pair of warm-up pants and a white tank top pulled over her Speedo. She must have come right from practice. Brent was grabbing her around the waist and lifting her in the air while she yelled at him to stop.

They saw me and Becca started to wave, but then spotted Larry at my side. I watched her arm slowly wilt. Her face wrinkled with confusion. Brent set Kelly down and whispered something in her ear. Kelly turned around. Her eyes looked ready to fall right out of her head onto the gym floor at the sight of me with my five-foot "partner."

I pushed through the crowd, feeling rather than seeing the faces turning in my direction. Larry lagged behind me like a reluctant appendage.

"Hi, guys," I said with a ghastly attempt at breeziness. I sipped at my drink. Becca's eyes were very round and Kelly's mouth hung slightly open. "Stop freaking out," I muttered out of the corner of my mouth.

"This is my cousin. See? It's perfect—doesn't violate the GNBP!"

Becca nodded, somewhat mechanically. "Yeah, brilliant," she echoed. Her eyes were fixed on Larry's sneakers. Someone had closed the gym doors and the air was positively tropical now. A droplet of sweat trickled down my spine.

"Hey, Val," Brent greeted me. "Hey . . ." I could see him realizing he didn't know Larry. "Hey," he finished. He stuck out his hand toward Larry. "Brent."

"Sorry," I broke in. "Brent, this is my—"

"Date." Larry stepped up too close to my side and shook Brent's hand with one of those double-clasp pumps, like he was some kind of politician. "Nice to meet you."

I stared at my cousin, thunderstruck. Larry's voice seemed to have dropped an entire octave, and instead of the half-asleep look, he now wore a self-assured smile. He suddenly bore a strong resemblance to Al Gore. He slid his eyes in my direction and suddenly I understood. I was going to pay for the loss of Assassin's Creed. Oh, I was going to pay.

Kelly shook her head. "Val, I thought you said this was your cousin . . . ?"

"Actually, that's just one of Val's little jokes," Larry broke in before I could respond. His voice carried over to the groups standing near us. People stopped talking and turned to look. I saw Willy standing on the edge of a group, his face stricken. Larry reached up and draped his arm manfully around my shoulders. "Val and I have been going out for a while now."

I hacked on my swallow of Diet Coke, snorting some up my nose in the process. I began coughing. Larry pounded me on the back helpfully. "Okay there, sweetheart?" he asked. "She's a little shy about the whole situation," he explained to the crowd of interested onlookers, including Kevin, who had now gathered around us.

I spluttered again violently, still trying to rid my lungs of Diet Coke droplets, and flapped one hand in the air, trying to communicate "Larry's a giant liar" with little success.

"You'll have to speak up, sweetheart," Larry said, extending his Al Gore smile to everyone around us. "Yes, we met at Burger King."

"*Burger King?*" Becca squeaked, her voice reaching an operatic level. I heard a few snickers from our attentive audience.

"Larry!" I finally cleared my throat enough to talk. I surreptitiously pinched his arm as hard as I could. "Shut up if you want to live to see fourteen," I whispered ferociously. He didn't even flinch.

"Yes, Val just loves Burger King, did you all know that? She can eat six Whoppers in a row." Larry waved an arm above his head as if to illustrate my imaginary fast-food appetite. With a sudden wave of nausea, I saw Dave step over to the crowd, a Prada-clad Taylor on his arm. Larry generously raised his voice to include them too. "Val's *so* in love with Burger King that she's actually thinking of working there, which I think would be a great choice for my little snook-ums." Larry wrapped his skinny arm a little tighter around my shoulders.

My voice seemed to have fled the scene. All I could do was open and close my mouth like a brain-damaged goldfish. Then I spotted a couple standing at the edge of the crowd. It was Adam, his eyes wide. He'd obviously heard everything Larry had said. Next to him, standing very close, was a tall blond girl wearing a white peasant blouse over a long green skirt.

"Larry, you're a liar," Kelly said. "You're Val's cousin, so stop saying you're her date." I threw Kelly an appreciative glance, but it was too late. Her words were drowned out in the sudden thump of salsa from behind me. I turned around. The dance teacher was now standing in front of the table, clapping his hands in rhythm. "All right, everybooody!" he called. "I'm Rick and this is just the start of our great night of daaancing!" He held his arms out at his sides and wiggled his hips.

"Oh, my dear God," Becca muttered next to me. Rick climbed off the stage and began circulating in the crowd of juniors and seniors, grabbing couples and spacing them out on the dance floor like so many chess pieces. I tried to hide behind Kelly as he came nearer to us, but before I could even blink, I was standing on a patch of empty gym floor, one hand on Larry's bony shoulder, the other clasping his hand. The top of his head came approximately to my chin.

"Larry, I'm going to scalp you," I whispered fiercely as Rick, now back on the stage, turned up the volume on the speakers. Conga drums resonated around us. "What were you doing?"

He grinned. "What, you're not a fan of Burger King?"

"No, I'm not! Just keep your mouth shut—"

"Now, everyone, listen up," Rick called, clapping his hands. "The first move we're going to do is called the box step. Very simple. Just step forward, gentlemen; ladies follow, now side, now back, now side . . ."

The couples around us began shuffling around decorously. I took a step forward but was suddenly jerked off balance as Larry, still flush with the success of his earlier joke, tightened his arm around my waist and tilted me backward in a low, dramatic dip. I found myself staring upside down at the lights hanging from the gym ceiling. "Ack," I just managed to gasp before Larry, snickering madly, was apparently overcome by his own sadism and dropped me with a crash.

I yelped as my tailbone made contact with the shiny, waxed floor. The couple nearest us glanced over in alarm. I smiled at them weakly as I picked myself and the shreds of my dignity off the floor. "You are scum, Larry," I hissed. I was happy to see he did look ever so slightly abashed.

"Ah, no, no, no." Rick had spotted the

debacle and was rushing over, waving his hands. "Very nice, young man, but yes, dips, we're not quite ready for dips. I'm glad you're enjoying yourself, though."

"Oh, we *are*, sir," Larry said loudly. "Very much."

"Shut up, shut up, shut up," I muttered under my breath like a mantra.

Rick returned to the stage and stopped the music momentarily. "All right!" he said, slapping his hands together and rubbing them like a happy chef. "Very nice! Let's add another element, shall we? Before you know it, you'll all be ready for *Dancing With the Stars*!" He laughed. Everyone stared at him, stone-faced, myself included.

"A twirl, just for fun. Gentlemen, just raise your lady's right hand above her head. Ladies, step away one step and twirl." Rick demonstrated with an imaginary partner. "Okay, now everyone will try it."

I pinned Larry with the most pointed stare I could muster. He gave me a huge toothy grin. I closed my eyes briefly, trying to summon my inner strength. It occurred to me that Larry could actually be beneficial. All the guys who had been bothering me at school would think I was off-limits.

For one nanosecond, I wondered if bringing Larry to prom would violate the GNBP. Then I shook my head violently. The heat of the gym must be getting to me.

"Do you have a tic or something?" Larry asked. His breath smelled like pizza. Before I could answer, he twirled me around so fast, I almost lost my balance all over again. I staggered slightly as I came to rest and was forced to pause, my hands on my knees, until the world around me stopped spinning.

"Very nice, very nice! Impressive enthusiasm!" Rick called across the room. "You there!"

I turned. He was pointing directly at us. *No, please.* I stared straight ahead, hoping that if I didn't look at him, he wouldn't be able to see me. But it didn't work any better than it had when I was three.

"Brown ponytail!" Rick was calling. "Would you and your partner mind demonstrating a few steps?"

I looked around to see if there might possibly be another brown ponytail in the vicinity. But no. There wasn't.

"Hey, that's us!" Larry sounded as if he'd been offered a free trip to 24-Hour Video-Game Land. He immediately started for the front of the room, dragging me behind him like a recalcitrant toddler.

God, haven't I suffered enough? I always thought I was a good person—you know, helped my mom, refrained from committing major felonies, that sort of thing. But apparently, I was now going to demonstrate salsa in front of two hundred of my classmates with my five-foot cousin as my partner.

Larry and I reached the riser, where Rick stood waiting, and mounted the steps. The audience of upturned faces swam before me like balloons in the sea. A little murmur ran through the crowd. "Yeah, Val!" someone yelled. It sounded like Kevin.

"Lovely work out there, you two." Rick slapped his hands together with relish. "Let's have you demonstrate a variation on the twirl, the in-and-out." He laughed merrily.

My heart quailed. I glanced over at Larry, who was ostentatiously rolling up his sleeves as if about to perform major surgery. This was just wrong on so many levels.

"Don't look so nervous, young lady!" Rick said. "This will be very easy. The young man—what is your name?" He looked at Larry questioningly.

"Lothario," Larry said. He pushed out his lips and narrowed his eyes in what I supposed was a "Hello, ladies" attitude. The audience below me erupted in laughter.

"*Lothario?*" I heard a guy in the front say to the girl next to him.

Rick didn't seem to notice anything amiss. "All right, Lothario. And who is your lovely partner?" He smiled at me, showing all his teeth.

"Val," I mumbled as quietly as possible.

"Hal?" Rick asked.

"*Val*," I said slightly louder, just as the music behind me swelled.

"Okay, so Hal and Lothario are going to demonstrate the in-and-out twirl," Rick informed the crowd.

"It's *Val*," I almost yelled, but he had already turned to Larry.

"Lothario, you'll want to stand just behind Hal, with your arm around her waist like this," Rick instructed. I cringed as Larry's arm crept across my midsection. Rick was still going on. "And then on the count of three, you'll want to take a step back, just *fling* her out, and then twirl and *pull* her back in. Ready? And one-two-three . . ."

Larry took a giant step back and with

what must have been all the strength in his skinny arm, threw me out across the riser like a slingshot. Unfortunately, at the end of the *fling*, he failed to keep hold of my hand. I skittered across the flimsy plywood floor, groping frantically for Larry's hand, which was now a good foot away from my own, and soared off the edge of the riser. I pinwheeled my arms wildly as I pitched headlong into space, only to fall directly on top of the vice principal, knocking him flat on the floor.

"Ooof!" Mr. Solis woofed. A loud "Ooooh" rose from the audience around us. You know the moment in every action movie when the scene goes into slow motion and all you can hear is the hero's heartbeat, like really loud and really slow, as he stares into the barrel of the gun aimed at him? And then he launches himself off into midair, shouting "Nooooo!" in slo-mo, all deep? Well, this was just like that.

For about five years, I stared pop-eyed into Mr. Solis's face, which was two inches from my own. His mouth opened and closed without sound, as if he were underwater. Then I snapped out of my trance. I rolled to the side, climbed to my feet, and gathering all the focus I had left, forced myself to smile calmly at the ring of fascinated eyes around me, as if tackling the vice principal on the gym floor were the most normal thing in the world. Kelly and Becca rushed up to me. Adam was following closely behind, minus his blond partner, as my stunned mind dimly noted. "Are you okay?" Becca whispered. I nodded. She put her arm around my shoulders. On my other side, Adam patted my upper arm. I gave him a grateful little smile.

Mr. Solis, his face now practically eggplant colored, got slowly and painfully to his feet. He stood for a moment, straightening his wrinkled gray suit jacket, then took out a large white handkerchief and mopped his streaming face. The gym was completely silent, except for the sound of his heavy breathing.

Up on the stage, Larry and Rick were standing frozen. Then Rick broke from his trance, gave Larry a shove, and nodded in my direction. Larry blinked and scrambled down off the stage, weaving his way through the crowd in my direction. Without warning, Adam dropped back and melted into the crowd. "Don't look at me, don't talk to me, don't come near me," I hissed through my teeth as Larry came near. He wisely faded back several feet behind me.

Mr. Solis looked around at the assembled crowd. "I think—" He stopped and cleared his throat. "Perhaps we might all go home a little early tonight." He waved his hand over us. "Dismissed."

No one moved.

He raised his voice. "Dismissed! Go home! Get a decent night's rest for once . . ." He turned toward the door, mumbling. People stepped aside as he passed by, making a little path in the silent crowd. All eyes followed his wide gray back as it passed the bleachers and disappeared through the blue metal doors.

Then, as if given a cue, everyone began milling around, talking loudly and gathering their backpacks to head out to the parking lot. I looked around for Adam, but he had faded back into the crowd. "You want a ride, Val?" Becca asked, her face still creased with concern. "You can just leave the Saab in the parking lot. No one would care."

I shook my head. "Thanks, guys. I have to drive my idiot date home. Call you later, okay?" I waved at them and pushed through the crowd, trying to ignore the stares and murmurs that followed me. I had almost reached the gym doors when I heard my name called.

I turned. Dave stood behind me, smiling a little and miraculously Taylor-less. I gritted my teeth, but even so, I could feel my heart rate zoom up. This was the first time I'd seen him alone since the breakup. I'd forgotten how dark his eyes were. Before I could say anything, he put a hand on my arm and pulled me into a shadowy place under the bleachers.

We faced each other. He was standing close enough for me to smell his aftershave— something woodsy. I folded my arms across my chest, resisting the urge to throw myself against his incredibly hot self. That was how I wound up with him in the first place.

I didn't say anything. He shuffled his feet. Behind us, crowds streamed out the gym doors, but we were alone under the bleachers. Finally, Dave spoke. "Val, I know we haven't talked really since, um, after spring break, but I, ah, wanted to tell you that I'm sorry if I hurt you. I never meant for things to happen this way. They just sort of . . . did."

I stared at him. My pulse began pounding in my ears. For a minute, I didn't trust myself to speak. *"They just sort of did?"* I struggled to keep my voice steady. *"That's* your reason for cheating on me out of nowhere?"

Dave's mouth hardened. He held up his hands. "Hey, Val, look, I was just trying to apologize here——"

All of the anger from the last month boiled up in me. "That is the crappiest apology I have ever heard. You're sorry *if* you hurt me? You *did* hurt me! You never meant to cheat on me? Then *why did you?"* Now I was almost shouting, my face only a few inches from his.

He backed up a few steps and glanced out at the gym nervously. "Keep your voice down, would you? I'm actually trying to be *nice.* But if you don't want to talk, that's cool." He let his hands drop to his sides. "I didn't know I was going to get yelled at for saying I'm sorry."

I just stared at him, my mouth hanging open. Who *was* this guy? The one who decided we should slide down the bunny slope on our butts, instead of on our skis? The one who spent all morning making a snowman with me in front of the cabin?

I closed my eyes and took several deep

breaths, concentrating on my breath going in and out of my nose, just like we learned in yoga. I willed myself not to commit an act of homicide right here in the school gym. I opened my eyes. Dave was gone.

I whirled around, only to see his back disappearing into the crowd. I watched him weave through the throngs of people until he reached the distant door. Taylor was waiting for him, fiddling with her giant gold handbag. She took his hand. He said something to her. She turned and stared at me. I gave her a huge, fake grin and a big wave. *He's all yours, chick. Have a great time. You two deserve each other.*

Larry was thumbing his phone silently when I opened the car door. He didn't even look up as the yellow dome light illuminated the interior. "You're lucky you're not walking," I said as I turned the key and, looking behind me, backed carefully out of the parking space.

"Whatever," he mumbled.

"Whatever? Are you serious?" I beeped at a car in front of me that was hanging out at a stop sign. "You tell heinous, stupid lies about me to the entire class, dump me on the floor, and throw me off the stage onto the vice principal, and *whatever* is all you can say?" I had officially entered screeching mode.

"Yeah, is that a problem for you?" he shouted back, his voice cracking on the last word. He stuffed his phone into his pocket and crossed his arms over his chest.

"It *is* a problem, you stupid little—," I yelled before I stopped myself. I was not going to let this devolve into a shouting match with idiot Larry.

We drove the rest of the way in black silence, Larry immobile in the passenger seat, radiating noxious rays of sullenness; myself hunched over the steering wheel, grinding my teeth, wondering at what speed you could throw someone out of a car without having them actually die. At Aunt Beth's, Larry slammed the car door as hard as he could and stalked up the walkway. Losing my iron grip on self-control, I rolled down the window. "Have fun with your stupid game!" I shouted. "Don't feel lame or anything, sitting at home by yourself!" Not very clever, but I felt better as soon as the words were out of my mouth. Larry turned around and gave me the finger, not noticing that Aunt Beth had opened the front door and seen the whole thing.

As I steered the car toward home, my thoughts turned back to the scene with Dave. It was like talking to him had exorcised something inside of me. If there had been any cell, any atom, that was hanging on to Dave, it was gone. I snapped on the radio and found "Girls Just Want to Have Fun" blaring from the speakers. I rolled down the windows and let the cool night air whisk through the car. "*Daddy dear, you know you're still number one, but girls just wanna have fu-un, oooh, girls just wanna have fun,*" I shouted into the dark night. I sang all the way home.

Thirteen

"Now, look, Val, just forget about the whole thing," Becca advised as she, Kelly, and I walked down the hall at school the next morning. "You were just attracting some bad vibes last night, that's all. You need to keep your mind on the GNBP." She stuck a cherry Blow Pop in her mouth and sucked on it noisily. "Just think how great Kelly is going to look in those purple heels."

Kelly smacked her on the shoulder. "What happened after you left?" she asked me.

I rummaged through the front pocket of my bag. "Well, I talked to Dave, did you know that?" I unzipped another pocket and dug around futilely. "Do either of you guys have any Advil?"

"What? You actually *talked* to him?" Kelly gasped. "How can you say that so casually?" She shook two Advil into my palm from a little white bottle.

"I'm not casual," I told her. We reached the open door of the calc room. Becca glanced at her watch.

"We have five minutes." We all sank down on the linoleum, our backs against the wall.

"So what did he say?" Becca asked. "I can't stand it—tell us!"

I shrugged. "He just said, basically, he was sorry if he hurt me—"

Kelly held up her hand. "Stop. He's sorry *if* he hurt you? He *did* hurt you!"

"I know, that's just what I said. And then he acted like I was hysterical just because I was defending myself." I leaned my head back against the wall. "I was so mad when we were talking, but I actually started feeling better on the way home. Like I have some closure now. I can see he's a jerk, finally, once and for all. So I can let him go."

"Yay!" Becca cheered. She leaned over and gave me a hug. "I'm so glad for you. Go, Val!"

"Thanks, babe." I hugged her back.

"Awesome show last night, Val." We looked up. Kevin walked past us into the calc room, but not without turning and giving me a big grin. I shuddered.

"Oh no, Val," Kelly muttered, looking at the end of the hall. I followed her gaze. Mr. Solis was striding toward us, a set of files clutched in his hand. Today his suit was wrinkled blue instead of wrinkled gray.

"Oh my God, I do not want him to see me," I whispered. "He smelled like spaghetti."

"Come on, get in the classroom, hurry," Becca whispered back, giggling. We grabbed our bags. Kelly and Becca swung theirs over their shoulders.

"Mine's stuck!" I said, tugging at the strap, which was snagged on a metal doorstop. Mr. Solis was getting closer. Becca's giggling grew louder as all three of us yanked at the bag strap. Now I could hear Mr. Solis's footsteps. "Don't look, don't look," I muttered. We all grew quiet and stared down at the bag as he passed by, his own eyes fixed firmly on the end of the hall.

I felt distinctly nervous that afternoon as I got ready to go to Sternwell's. Had Adam decided that I was completely crazy, prancing around with Larry like that, then falling off the riser? I put on an army green tank top and a pair of painty khakis and got in the Saab. I stopped at a 7-Eleven on the way and bought two Hershey's bars. Just in case Adam didn't want to paint with a crazy girl, maybe I could bribe him.

It was hot and muggy. The sky was whitish with a disk of harsh sun glaring through. I could see flies buzzing in a little cloud over the Dumpster on the corner as I approached the mural. Adam was squatting near our supplies, which we kept piled under a blue tarp at the side of the building. He was making careful piles of our paintbrushes, his face downturned.

"Hey," I said. "What's up?"

He glanced at me briefly, and then returned to his sorting. "Nothing much." That was it.

"Do you want some help?" I crouched down next to him.

He shrugged. So it was true. He thought I was a weird, vice-principal-attacking freak who was dating a five-foot-tall thirteen-year-old.

I tried again. "Hey, I got us a snack on the way here." I pulled the chocolate bars out of my pocket. He glanced at them.

"I'm not really that hungry right now. Thanks, though. Listen," he said, rising to his feet. "We're out of a ton of stuff— blue paint, turpentine, and someone stole a bunch of our clean brushes. I told Sarah I'm going down to Mason's Art Supply to stock up, okay? I'll be back soon." He turned on his heel and started toward the street where his car was parked.

"Okay," I said to his back. I suddenly felt very alone standing there in the weedy lot by myself.

"You can go home if you want. I probably won't be back for a while," he said over his shoulder, digging in his pocket for his keys. He turned to the car.

"Can I come with you?" I shouted on impulse.

He wrestled with the door, and then wrenched it open in a shower of rust. "If you want." He slid behind the wheel as I climbed in beside him.

As before, the intermittently scraping tailpipe made conversation nearly impossible, but this time there wasn't any light banter anyway. Adam drove with one hand on the wheel, the other resting on the gearshift, staring straight ahead out the windshield. I folded my hands on my lap and watched the Taco Bells and liquor stores slide by. I was acutely aware of Adam's every movement next to me, as if I'd suddenly sprouted invisible antennae. Finally, I couldn't stand the silence one second longer.

I took a deep breath. "So that was so crazy at the dance lesson——," I began.

"Yeah, what was up with that?" Adam's hands tightened convulsively on the wheel. I glanced over. His knuckles were white.

"Listen, I can explain everything," I rushed ahead. "I'm not crazy, I swear, even though I know it really seems like I am." Here I let out a little hyena laugh, which did not do much to help my case.

"You know, you could have just told me you already had a partner when I asked you at the co-op the other day," he said, his words short and clipped.

"Well, that's what I wanted to explain about——"

He glanced over at me and then back at the windshield. I could see the muscles of his jaw clenched. "You could have just told me the truth. The one thing I can't stand is lying."

"Listen, Adam, that guy was my *cousin* Larry. My aunt was like totally begging me to take him so that he could learn dancing. It was a favor to her, that's all."

He glanced over. "Really?"

"Yeah." I paused. "To tell you the truth, he's not really my type." I grinned at Adam so he'd be sure and get the joke.

He laughed. We drove in a comfortable silence for a few minutes, then Adam reached his hand behind him and felt his back pockets. "Darn." He glanced over at me.

"What?"

"Do you mind taking a side trip? I think I left my wallet at my house. It's right near here."

"Sure, that's fine," I said. I watched as he steered us through the suburban streets. The houses shrank from McMansions set far back from the road to comfortable frame houses with large, fenced lawns to finally a quiet street of small brick bungalows. He killed the engine in front of a tidy house with white trim. Plain white curtains fluttered from the open windows.

"My parents are still at work," Adam told me, climbing from the car. He unlocked the door and I followed him into the small, dim living room. As my eyes adjusted from the bright light of outdoors, I found myself staring at a giant nude in oil that hung on the living room wall right in front of me. Adam saw my surprise.

"My mom paints too," he explained, throwing his keys on the coffee table. "And this stuff is my dad's." He pointed and I turned to see a row of large abstract horse sculptures standing in the tiny dining nook.

"Do you like it that your parents are artists too?" I asked. "Is it annoying?"

He shrugged. "Sometimes. They have their own ideas about what I should be painting and *I* have my own ideas about what I should be painting. But most of the time, we get along." He stepped into the kitchen, which was about four feet away, and rummaged through a drawer for a second, then slammed it shut. "I must have left the wallet in my room. I'll be right back."

"Don't worry about me." I perched on the edge of one of the wooden dining chairs.

He disappeared down a short hallway. I rested my elbow on the table. It was very quiet in the house. The only sound was the ticking of the kitchen clock. I stared at the salt and pepper shakers on the table, which looked like two little people embracing, the salt white ceramic and the pepper black.

I shifted my seat on the chair. Adam was taking forever. I got up and peered down the hallway. I could hear shuffling from one of the three open doors. "Adam?" I called.

"Yeah," he called back. "I'm in here."

I walked down the hall and stood in the doorway. The only sign it was a bedroom was a mattress heaped with rumpled blankets on the floor. Several drop cloths were spread out in one corner, where an easel stood near the window. Squeezed, empty tubes of oils cluttered the windowsills along with mason jars filled with worn paintbrushes. Dozens of canvases were stacked against the wall. Some of them were facing backward, but I caught a glimpse of a bright blue figure, and a landscape done in browns and oranges, and what looked like a pair of giant yellow lips. Adam was standing half-buried in a closet, flinging flannel shirts and jeans behind him onto the floor.

"I think I left it in these jeans," he mumbled. "Aha!" He turned around, holding up a brown leather wallet triumphantly. "I knew it was there." With his foot, he swept all the dirty clothes back into the closet and shut the door.

"I like all your paintings," I told him, looking around. "This is like a real artist's studio."

He shrugged. "It's okay. I wish the windows were bigger. But Mom is really cool to let me paint in here—I'm not always so neat when I work, in case you haven't noticed," he said, leading the way from the room.

"Nooo, I've never noticed that," I teased. He turned around and grinned at me, and I grinned back.

I couldn't help glancing in the other rooms as we passed by—a little bathroom, his parents' room with a big bed. I peered in the doorway of what looked like an office, with an Oriental rug on the floor and a computer desk in the corner. Boxes were strewn all over, with paper stacked on the floor and clothes draped over the desk chair. Then I did a double take and skidded to a stop. Hanging on one wall was the most beautiful gown I had ever seen. It was floor-length dark blue silk, flowing like water down the white-painted wall. The shoulder straps were wide bands of silk. Cream-colored chiffon was draped softly across the bodice, and fell in swathes to the hem. "Wow," I breathed. Adam turned around and followed my gaze.

"Oh yeah," he said. "That was my grandmother's. My mom was sorting some attic stuff this weekend. It's nice, right?"

"Nice!" I smacked him playfully on the shoulder. "What a typical guy. It's gorgeous! Wow, and vintage too." I paused. "Can I see it?"

He shrugged. "Sure." He took the dress off the wall and handed me the padded hanger.

The cool silk slid through my fingers and shimmered in the filtered sunlight from the window. A faint scent of long-ago jasmine wafted up to me. I held the hanger up to my shoulders. The hem fell perfectly to my toes. "Look," I said to Adam. "It's my size."

"You're right." He looked me up and down. "You look good in it."

His voice was casual, but something about his gaze made me drop my eyes. My heart gave a little jump. Quickly, I replaced the hanger on the wall. "Oops," I said with a moronic giggle as one of the straps slid off. I fixed it, and then walked rapidly from the room, not looking at Adam as I brushed by him.

We were quiet in the car on the way to the art store. I was glad for the randomly scraping tailpipe mixing with the Yeah Yeah Yeahs song blaring from the tinny speakers. After about ten minutes, Adam turned onto a busy street lined with stores on both sides. "This is it," he said, pulling up in front of an art shop with a sign shaped like a palette. Wooden modeling mannequins filled the window, along with blank canvases, cases of oil paints, and huge jars of brushes.

Adam held the door open for me and a bell tinkled overhead. It was quiet inside, and the air smelled of turpentine overlaid with the spicy aroma of books and paper. The white-haired proprietor perched on a high stool behind the counter at the back, reading a heavy, blue-bound book. He glanced over his half-glasses at us and nodded.

"Cool place," I whispered to Adam. I felt like I should whisper for some reason, even though it wasn't a library.

"Yeah, I know," he murmured back. "Hey, look at these prints over here. You've got to see this one by Diego Rivera. It's my favorite painting in the entire world." He grabbed my hand. His warm, rough palm rasped against mine. I inhaled sharply. This was the first time he'd touched me, except to shake my hand that night in the garden. I wasn't prepared for the shiver that zinged through my body.

Adam didn't seem to notice my odd reaction to his touch. He pulled me over to a bin full of cardboard-mounted prints wrapped in plastic. I stood beside him, gripping the cold metal edge of the rack as he rifled through the stack.

"This one." He pulled out a painting showing part of a factory, dark red and yellow, against a blue sky. "Isn't that incredible? The way the colors contrast? It's like what I'm trying with the mural, except it's a thousand times better, of course."

Something in his voice made me look at him more closely. His eyes were sparkling and his cheeks were a little flushed. This painting really meant something to him. I examined it more closely.

"Wow, you're right," I said. "The blue and red look amazing together." And it was true—the deep burnt red-orange of the building popped against the flat periwinkle of the sky.

"Now, *this* one, on the other hand . . ." He

pulled a print of a medieval painting from the bin. "This one reminds me of you."

"What?" I laughed. "Give me that!" I pulled it out of his hand. A woman draped in gauzy robes perched on a tree root in a deep forest. Her slender oval face was alert as she gazed at a baby Cupid, who was looking up at her in a questioning way.

"Oh, I see, so are *you* Cupid?" I teased, pointing to the little figure. I was gratified to see him blush.

"Well, *this* one reminds me of *you*," I told him. I pulled out a print of a pen-and-ink drawing depicting a very old man perched on a tree stump and clutching a walking stick. His face was a mass of wrinkles.

"Hey!" Adam protested. "All right, fine. You asked for it." He flipped rapidly through the prints, and then pulled out a still life of a single egg resting upright on a yellow table. He showed it to me.

I snorted laughter. "An egg? I remind you of an *egg*?"

He sheepishly dropped the print back into the rack. "Yeah, I couldn't find a better insult." He moved along the shelves of art books, trailing his finger along the bindings, then stopped and pulled out a large book of Richard Avedon photographs.

He motioned me over. "Here, check these out," he said. I put down the modeling mannequin I had been fiddling with and leaned over. He flipped through the haunting black-and-white photos.

"Look at that one." I pointed to a picture of a Native American man.

"Yeah," he said. But something about his voice made me look up. He was staring at my face, not at the photo. I realized all of a sudden that we were so close, the hairs on my arm felt like they were standing on end. Adam moved a half inch closer. I didn't breathe. The soft fabric of his T-shirt brushed my bare shoulder. I jumped like I'd been burned. His breath smelled like toothpaste. A long moment spun out, while I wondered if he could actually hear my heart pounding. Then Adam abruptly stared back at the book, his cheeks flaming red. I took a step away and let out a long, shaky breath, wiping my hands on my khakis. My palms were dripping sweat. I turned away and stared at the titles on the wall opposite us. *Early Etruscan Sculpture*, I read meaninglessly. My brain didn't seem capable of processing much more.

I heard a thump behind me and turned around. Adam was throwing cans of paint into his basket, seemingly at random. He moved down to the paintbrushes hanging with military neatness on a pegboard against one wall. As I watched, he rapidly selected half a dozen of different sizes, then piled the whole lot on the counter in front of the white-haired man. Adam said something to the man, who bent down and lifted a large can of turpentine from under the counter.

Adam loaded everything into a big, flat cardboard box and staggered toward me. "Okay, I think this is everything," he mumbled, without meeting my gaze. I nodded mechanically and trailed after him out the door.

The bright sunshine hit us like a jolt of reality after the cool, dim interior of the shop. I shook my head, feeling as if I had been awakened from a spell. As I turned toward Adam to make a little joke or something, anything to restore normalcy between us, I noticed two familiar figures walking toward us. I squinted down the sidewalk. It was Becca and Kelly.

"Oh my God," I said. My muscles tensed,

as if I'd been doing something wrong. Which was crazy, because I hadn't.

"What?" Adam turned around.

"Hey there!" Becca said as they approached. She was wearing the same outfit I'd seen her in at school—knee-length gray wool shorts and a pink oxford shirt.

"What's up, Val?" Kelly said. She was still in her swimming warm-ups, her wet hair pulled back in a loose knot. Her eyes darted from me to Adam and back again.

"Hi! I didn't expect to see you guys." I tried to sound casual but it was coming out loud. *Relax, Val. You're acting like you got caught sneaking out of the house.* I forced what I hoped was a relaxed smile. "What are you doing all the way out here?"

Both of them stared at me. "Dad's store is right here," Becca said deliberately, as if talking to a four-year-old. "Remember?" She pointed to the lighting showroom a couple of doors down. "I was just picking up some documents for him before I dropped Kels off . . ." She trailed off, her eyes darting from Adam's face to my red one. Her eyes narrowed. There was a little silence. I shifted my weight from one foot to the other.

"How's the mural going, anyway?" Kelly asked, breaking the silence. She was smiling broadly.

"It's going great," Adam said. "We're actually back on schedule. Val's helped me catch up. I thought my boss was going to handcuff me to the wall before." He grinned and rolled his eyes.

"But Sarah wouldn't actually do that, right, Adam?" Becca said. "You and she seem to have a really *special* relationship." She looked straight at Kelly when she said these last words.

Adam nodded pleasantly and shifted the box with our painting supplies to his other arm. "Yeah. Sarah's great. I'm going to be in her wedding this summer."

Becca's eyes widened. "What?"

"I said—"

She cut Adam off. "She's getting married? So she's with someone else?" Her voice was growing louder. We all stared at her.

Adam looked utterly confused. "Uh . . . yeah. Her fiancé."

"Oh, I see," Kelly said. "We understand the situation now perfectly." She smiled at Becca, who looked away.

"Um, girls?" I looked from one friend to

the other. "So it was great seeing you, but we really have to get back now, so I'll——"

"Oh, Val, I forgot. Your mom wanted me to come take you home. She needs your help, um, making dinner." Becca grabbed my hand and started hauling me down the sidewalk.

"Dinner? But Mom has a meeting tonight." I struggled to free my hand. "She said she wouldn't be home until nine."

Becca shifted her grasp to my wrist and continued tugging. "Oh. That's right. She wants you to make dinner for your dad. Come on! We're going to be late."

I looked over my shoulder. "Bye, Adam. See you tomorrow." He waved.

"Bye, Adam!" Kelly trilled. "It was *so* nice seeing you again!" She waved so hard she rose up on her tiptoes.

"You told me he was with that girl Sarah," Becca muttered as she shoved me into the passenger seat of the Saab.

"I did not," I corrected her. "You told *me* he was with her, in the car coming back from Sternwell's. Remember? And he's not. She's just a friend, like he said." I felt like I had regained my equilibrium. I didn't have any reason to be nervous. I was just a little thrown by seeing the girls unexpectedly. "Why does it matter, Bec? We're just working together."

"*You know* why it matters," she hissed. "You're working alone with a single guy!"

I rolled my eyes. "We're. Just. Friends. Can I spell it out for you? F-R-I—"

"That's right," Kelly piped up from the back. "I for one think it's great that Val has such a sweet guy to hang out with."

"Shut up, Kel." Becca turned and shot Kelly a look.

"Can you both get it through your heads once and for all that he is not my type?" I said. "Remember? We went through this. Arty dudes, no."

"But don't you think he's kind of cute, Val?" Kelly leaned forward in her seat. "I've heard guys who draw are great kissers."

"Really?" I said, momentarily distracted. Then I shook my head violently. *Focus, Val, focus. Kelly's just trying to throw you off your game.*

Kelly smiled with satisfaction, as if she could read my mind. "You know," she said to the car at large, "I think my red silk dress would just contrast too much with those diamonds, so I'm going to go with basic black instead."

"Dream on, my darling. The GNBP is still going strong." I leaned over the seat and murmured in Kelly's ear. "I think you'd better be thinking of buying some panty hose to go with those heels of yours. They'll match your purple dress *so* well."

She swatted at my head and I laughed, then sat back with satisfaction for the rest of the ride home.

Fourteen

The next day at school, I was heading to our usual lunch tree, anticipating the chicken-breast-Swiss-cheese-Granny-Smith sandwich in my backpack, when I froze halfway across the lawn. A third person was sitting under our lunch tree with Becca and Kelly. I could tell by the shoulders that it was a guy. Great. It was probably that rugby guy Kelly was obsessed with. Looking at that zit on his nose was totally going to ruin my appetite.

Becca and Kelly looked up as I approached. I waved and the guy turned around. I almost pitched forward facefirst onto the grass. It was Adam. "Hey there," he said, smiling.

"Val!" Kelly patted the spot between her and Adam. "Isn't this awesome?"

"Hi, Adam." I gingerly lowered myself to the grass as if there might be a land mine nearby and unwrapped my sandwich. "Um . . . I thought seniors usually went out at lunchtime."

"They do," Adam said. He looked supremely comfortable, sitting cross-legged on the grass, his knees poking out like a grasshopper's, munching on what looked like a peanut-butter-and-jelly. "But I ran into Kelly in the hall and she invited me to eat with you guys. I was just going to work in the art room, anyway."

"*Such* a weird coincidence since we saw you guys yesterday, right?" Kelly chirped. "But Adam is such a sweetie that I was like, we all should hang out sometime! Right, Adam?" She flashed him a huge grin.

Adam looked pleased, if slightly confused. "Sure. It was good seeing you girls too."

Becca snorted. Her nostrils were flared—always a sign she was mad. At Kelly? Adam? *Me?* I tried to make eye contact but she was gazing pointedly in the opposite direction. My eyes darted to Kelly. She was calmly spooning up strawberry yogurt.

"Well, I don't know how you guys are going to get the mural done if all you ever do is shop," Becca snapped.

"Like we said, we just needed some more supplies," I pointed out. Adam nodded assent.

"It seemed more like hanging out to me." She shook a bottle of water at me.

My eyes widened. "Thanks, Mom," I said. "Am I grounded, or what?"

Kelly giggled. "What's wrong, Becs? Are you jealous of Val?"

Becca narrowed her eyes at Kelly and looked away again.

Adam looked back and forth among all of us, as if he were watching the exotic ritual of some foreign peoples.

Kelly turned back to Adam. "So, Adam, where did you learn to paint?" she asked, leaning in confidentially and gazing at him as if he were Zac Efron.

Adam bit noisily into an apple. "Nowhere in particular," he said between crunches. "I've always liked art and stuff. The mural's going to be awesome when it's done, right, Val?"

"Yeah, Val's so good at stuff like that!" Kelly burbled before I could answer.

"She *is*?" Becca suddenly barked. "I don't

think she is. She's just doing it for her project, Kelly. Right, Val?"

Everyone turned to me.

This situation needed some serious triage. I got to my feet, stuffing my lunch wrappings into my bag. "Becs, I left my calc text in the Beemer this morning. Can you let me in?"

Adam got up also. "I probably should head over to the art room," he said, brushing off his jeans. "Pencil drawings of fruit bowls await." He grinned at us and started to turn away, then stopped as if something had occurred to him. "By the way, Val, do you want to go with me on a scouting expedition later? I want to go check out some of this graffiti art I heard about a ways out of town. It's on an old water tank."

I glanced uncomfortably at Becca's and Kelly's avid faces. Kelly gave me an encouraging little nod. Becca looked away pointedly. "Sure, why not?" I said to Adam. "Anything *for the project*." I aimed these last words at Becca.

"Cool. I'll pick you up at seven, okay?"

"Okay." I hauled Becca away. Halfway to the parking lot, I grabbed her arm and pulled her behind a large honeysuckle bush.

"Okay, what's up?" I said, folding my arms across my chest.

She widened her eyes. "I don't know what you're talking about, Val. Have you been out in the sun too much?"

I exhaled through my nose. "Nice try. You're being totally nasty to Adam! What's the deal? I thought you liked him. At least, that's what it seemed like when you were pushing me to paint with him."

She threw out her arms. "I *thought* you were just working on a project! But it looks to me like you've been working on a whole lot else too. You only have a week left of the GNBP—don't lose it now!"

I narrowed my eyes. "Oh, I see." I rocked back on my heels. "You think I have a crush on Adam. Well, you're sounding just a little paranoid, to tell you the truth."

She leaned forward so much that our noses were almost touching. "Oh, I'm just paranoid, huh? I'm not stupid, you know. I can tell when two people are attracted to each other."

"There is *nothing* going on with Adam and me," I barked. But as I spoke, a little bell rang somewhere in the back of my mind. I ignored it. "Don't you know me? Do you actually think I'd sabotage the GNBP—my own plan—just for some random guy?" I paused. "The whole point of the GNBP was to get away from romance, remember?"

Becca shrugged. "Whatever. I only know what I see, that's all." She stepped out from behind the bush. "Do you really need your calc text? Because I'm dying to pee before the bell rings."

I shook my head. "No, go ahead." I sank onto a boulder behind me as her footsteps faded down the walkway. The stone was hard under my rear, but I ignored it. I leaned my head on my hands and took a deep breath. Becca was really full of herself. Thinking that she could always figure me out. For a moment, the image of Adam's face close to mine flashed through my head and I shivered. Then I closed my eyes and concentrated on shoving it firmly away.

The sun was already setting when we pulled up to the abandoned water tank that evening. The big round structure sat alone, directly on the ground, starkly outlined against the soft violet sky. It was surrounded by a field of long dry grass, tinted pink and orange from the fading sun. Far off to either side, I could see the boxy, nondescript outlines of nameless warehouses. There was no one else around. Adam parked on a little patch of gravel and killed the engine. I got out of the car and slammed my door. The sound echoed like a shot in the silence. My feet scrunched on the gravel as I walked to the edge of the field. I followed the small dark shape of a killdeer as she swooped across the grass, calling shrilly.

The wind blew sharply and I shivered as Adam came up.

"Are you cold?" he asked, looking down at me.

"A little," I admitted. "It seems colder out here."

"Hold on." I heard his footsteps scrunch away, then the bang of the car door, then footsteps returning. Something soft draped around my shoulders. I looked down to see a gray zip-up hoodie. I poked my arms through the sleeves and looked up at Adam. "Thanks. This is perfect." It was warm from the car and smelled faintly of wood smoke.

He smiled at me. "It's the veteran of many campfires. Come on, let's go check out the water tank."

Together we tramped across the brown, rustling grass, the wind tousling our hair. The air smelled fresh, as if we were miles from the city. "I thought I might get some inspiration on colors from some of this graffiti art that's out here," Adam explained as we walked. "I've always heard the stuff is amazing."

We neared the water tank. Now I could see it was made of a kind of rough brown stucco. On this side, the surface was blank, with no sign of drawings. We circled around to the back. "All right . . . ," Adam breathed. Huge swathes of color spread from the round top of the tank to the bottom edge partially obscured by grass. Blue, red, orange, yellow, all laid on with spray paint so thick it looked like oil. Big, poufy swirls of white outlined with black were scattered across the colors. They may have been words, but they were so stylized I couldn't tell.

We walked around for a long time, with Adam carefully examining the colors and occasionally taking a picture with his phone. The sun was now a red half orb burning up the horizon. Finally I sat down cross-legged on the grass a few feet way from the tank and gazed out across the field, idly pulling up blades of stiff grass with my fingers. Adam came to sit next to me. He looped his arms around his updrawn knees. This close to the ground, I could smell the rich scent of the earth mixed with the hay aroma of the dry grass. Neither of us said anything, but the silence wasn't uncomfortable. I plucked at a purple meadow flower near my fingers. "Look," I said to Adam. "What's this called?"

He looked down. "I don't know—some kind of a thistle?" Then suddenly he laid his hand on top of mine, which was resting on my knee. I stared at his hand like it was an archeological specimen. It was very warm and all I could think about was how cold my own hand was.

"Val," he said, his voice low and husky. I didn't dare look up. "Val," he said again, more insistently. He put his finger under my chin and gently turned my face toward his. I could hear my pulse pounding in my head and a curious roaring noise, as if I were holding a conch shell to my ear. The thought that this situation was one iota away from violating the GNBP flitted through my mind, and then was gone.

Adam leaned over. I could feel the warmth of his body and the muscles of his shoulder pressing into mine. His eyes were huge, filling up my field of vision. He slid his warm, rough hand across my back and up to the nape of my neck. I shivered. He bent his dark head toward mine. I felt my eyes close and my lips part. For an instant, his lips hovered above mine.

Then, with a supreme force of will, I opened my eyes and pulled away. His eyes flew open also. "Adam, I can't do this," I panted, scrambling to my feet. My heart was galloping in my chest. "I—I want to . . . but I can't."

"Val, wait." Adam rose to his feet and reached out his hand. "I'm sorry. I was just . . ." He looked at me a moment, then took a deep breath. He shook his head as if clearing out cobwebs. "I don't know. I'm sorry. Let's go back."

The sun was gone and a soft, deep purple was settling over the grasses as we tramped back. Ahead, I could see Adam's car crouching alone at the edge of the field, like a dog waiting for us to return. Adam's arm swung next to mine. It seemed like the most natural thing in the world to just reach out and clasp it in mine, but I didn't. I couldn't, I reminded myself. No matter how much I wanted to.

Fifteen

On Monday of the next week, I arrived at Sternwell's, rounded the familiar corner, and stopped short. There in front of me spread the mural in swathes of rich orange, red, and blue. The fire-flower burst from the center, its black feathers almost floating on the wall.

"Wow," I breathed, stepping back almost to the curb to take in the whole effect.

"Looks pretty good, doesn't it?" Adam's voice came from behind me.

I jumped back and bumped into his warm, broad chest. I swung around. "I didn't know you were already here."

"Yeah." He looked at me a moment, then stepped away and picked up a brush. "My last class was canceled."

"It's so weird, I just came around the corner and realized we're, like, almost *done*." I gestured at the wall. "I just felt like we'd be painting forever, you know?"

Adam grinned and nodded. "I know. I thought the same thing. Sarah was just looking at it before you came. She's really pleased. There's just this last bit at the bottom and the border to do. Like maybe two more days of work."

"Really," I said slowly.

He nodded. Then we looked at each other and I wondered if he was thinking the same thing I was—only two more days of working together. Then it was all over.

Adam abruptly turned away and picked up a fine, pointy brush. "This bottom piece shouldn't take too long." He indicated a long strip of brown at the bottom.

"Yeah, it's almost done." I knelt next to him in the grass. We painted together in silence for a long time. I was concentrating on following the tricky outline on one edge when I noticed that Adam had stopped painting. He was sitting back on his heels, rapidly tapping his paintbrush on the wall, staring blankly in front of him.

"Adam?" I nudged him. "Are you okay?"

He faced me. "Val," he said hoarsely. "I have to ask you something."

I stopped painting, which was a good idea since my hands had suddenly started shaking. I couldn't look at him. Instead, I fixed my eyes on the ground where a fuzzy gray caterpillar was moving through the grass blades like a mobile piece of dryer lint.

Adam inhaled. "Listen, I have to say this fast or I won't get it out." He stared straight ahead of him. The words came out in a rush as he exhaled. "This has been, like, an amazing month working with you, and I think we have a lot of fun together, but lately, I've been feeling like maybe there's something more between us."

I looked up and opened my mouth, but he gently laid his fingers across my lips. "Wait, I have to get through this."

I subsided.

He went on. "The other night at the water tank was really special. I know it ended kind of weird, but I don't think we should just let this go when it seems like we really have something together. And—" He took a huge breath and the rest of the words spilled out all smushed together. "I know this is totally the wrong time, but maybe do you think you want to go to prom with me? You know, as my, like, date?" His voice squeaked on the last word. He lapsed into silence, gripping his paintbrush so hard his knuckles were white.

I froze, my mind spinning. Just to get away from his gaze, I rose to my feet and dunked my paintbrush in our bucket of water. Every fiber of me wanted to tell Adam yes. But how could I? The end of the GNBP was still a week away. I looked at him silently.

"I'll take that as a no, then." He got up and walked away a few steps, turning his back. I watched the stiff, hurt set of his shoulders and felt like I might throw up.

He turned back and folded his arms. "Who are you going with, then?" he asked. I could tell he was trying to control his voice.

"Um, no one," I mumbled. I stared at my painty hands.

"But you are going." It wasn't a question. His eyes bore into me like they were going to drill right into my soul. I nodded helplessly.

"Well, maybe," I said, talking quickly now, as if I could cover up all the hurt with words. "I mean, I don't know for sure, but I might go stag, even though Becca and Kelly have dates, or you know, just, um, stay home because prom's kind of lame when you really think about it—"

"Whatever." The one word stopped my babbling like a cork in a bottle. "If you don't want to go with me, you should just say so." His voice was calmer now, but also colder.

"No, Adam, wait," I pleaded. Even though I knew I shouldn't, I took his hand as we stood in the sunshine. I couldn't help it. "It's not that. I *do* want to go with you. I just, um, can't. That's it. I don't know what else to say."

He jerked his hand out of mine. "What you really mean is that you're embarrassed to go with me." His voice rose. "Why don't you just be honest and say it?"

"No! That's not true at all."

"Then what?"

I sighed. "I can't tell you. Okay? Stop asking me!" My voice was louder than I intended and I saw Adam's face shut down as if a door had been slammed closed.

"Fine. I won't ask. Not now—not ever." He tossed his paintbrush into the water bucket and, spinning around, stalked across the grass and around to the front of the coffeehouse. A moment later, I heard the slam of the Volvo door, and then the scraping screech of the tailpipe as he drove away, leaving only the faint twittering of the sparrows on the sidewalk and the distant rumble of traffic. I stood frozen in the sunlight, still clutching my wet paintbrush.

Somehow, I managed to get myself into the car and home. Thank God both Mom and Dad were still at work. I even made it up the stairs and into the shower before I started crying, which I think is a pretty good achievement.

In the steamy bathroom, I leaned against the tile wall and let the hot water pound the back of my neck. Adam's wounded eyes kept swimming up in front of me.

I cried in the shower until the hot water ran out, then wrapped my hair in a towel with every intention of drying it, putting on some pajamas, and forgetting all about Adam, prom, the mural, Sternwell's, and No-Boyfriend Plans that were supposed to fix my life, not mess it up even more. Maybe a first-class ticket to Paris would be a better option.

But then the thought of never seeing Adam again (because I'd be living in Paris) made me sob even louder. I rolled over in bed and reached for my phone. Still sniffling, I speed-dialed Becca.

"Dude, Logan is here," she stage-whispered as soon as she picked up the phone. "Not a good time."

I couldn't help myself. "It's all a big meeesss!" I blubbered, snotting all over the receiver.

"Oh my God, what is it?" she asked, sounding alarmed. "Did something happen with Dave, or—"

I rolled back over and mashed my face into the pillow. "It's not Dave," I choked out. "Hold on." I heaved myself off the bed, noting the huge wet place on the pillow, and stumbled into the bathroom, where I grabbed the Kleenex box, and then retreated to my bed again. I pulled back the comforter and, holding my Kleenex, climbed under the covers with the phone. I pulled the comforter up over my head and tucked the phone between my ear and the pillow.

"Val? Val?" Becca was saying.

"I'm here," I snuffled.

"What's wrong?"

"Is Logan still there?"

"No, I told him it was my mom on the phone saying she was coming home early. He got out of here really fast. So what's the matter?"

I took a long wavering breath, blew my nose, and poured out the whole, awful story: the chemistry between me and Adam, the weirdness about the dance lesson, tension at graffiti tower, and finally, what had happened this afternoon.

"I really, really want to go to prom with him," I finished, surrounded by wads of damp tissue. "But it's not even that the GNBP isn't over until after prom. The problem is that—"

"You really like him, and not just as a boy toy," Becca finished for me.

I blinked and sat up. "Yeah. How'd you know?"

She sighed into my ear. "Val, it's so obvious. I've known for days. It was written all over you when we saw you at the art store, and then the day we sat with him at lunch just confirmed it. I'm not blind, you know."

"But this wasn't supposed to happen! I'm not done with the GNBP!" I wailed. Now the comforter was smothering me. I threw it off and lay flat on the bed with my arms and legs spread out. "But I feel awful keeping secrets from him. I don't know." I thrashed back and forth. "I mean, at first it was all about the GNBP and getting away from school. But now it's more than that—a lot more."

Becca sighed. "Look, why don't you just forget the GNBP? Who cares, anyway? Just go be with Adam."

"What!" I sprang off the bed as if it had suddenly become a nest of snakes. "Are you saying I should just *quit* the GNBP? What about our bet? What about the dress and the earrings?"

"So?"

"So! I thought you were supporting me." I leaned my forehead against the cool glass of the window and stared out at the neat, silent backyard.

"I *am*. Look, Val, I'm your best friend, right?"

"Right."

"And you know I love you like crazy, right?"

I sighed. "Of course. Where are you going with this?"

"Well, you're not going to like this," Becca said. "But I have to tell you I think it's incredibly dumb to give up this awesome guy for a bet. You're insanely stubborn."

"Thanks for the advice, Ms. Relationship Guru 2010. *I* think I need to just forget Adam and move on."

Becca lapsed into silence. I strained but I couldn't even hear her breathing. I pulled the phone away from my ear and looked at the screen. Still connected.

"Becca?"

More breathing. Then she said, "Sorry, I was just thinking about something. Okay, yeah, you're right. You probably should just put this whole thing behind you. The GNBP lives on! Right?" Her voice had changed from somber to perky.

"Right," I said, confused at the sudden shift. "That's what I'm thinking."

"Okay—hey, I have to go. Talk to you tomorrow." Before I could respond, she hung up. For a long time, I stood still in the middle of the room. My mind was boiling. But as my brain slowly cooled, I could see that the solution I had proposed—just forget Adam and move on with the GNBP— was actually now my biggest problem.

Sixteen

Friday night. *Bzz. Bzz.*

I reached one arm out from under the covers and slapped blearily at my alarm clock. "Shut up," I muttered at it. But the buzzing sound continued. I stuck my head out from the tangled covers and stared at the clock. Two thirty. My phone was vibrating on my bedside table. I grabbed at it and knocked it onto the floor.

"Oooh," I groaned, as only someone who is woken up at two thirty can, and leaned over to fish the phone out from under the bed. I held the screen up to my face. Kelly.

I flipped it open. "Wha?" I managed, sinking back onto the pillow. No one was there. I pulled the phone away and stared at the screen again. *Put clothes on and be outside in five minutes,* the text read.

I stared at the phone for several more moments, as if it were a genie lamp that might give me more information. Finally, I threw back the covers and heaved myself out of bed. I shivered as the cool air in the room hit my sweat-coated body. My night's sleep hadn't exactly been restful.

I stumbled around in the dark, tripping over various pieces of furniture, until I found my track pants. I pulled them on, stuffed my hair under my OSU baseball cap, and gingerly opened my door. All was dark and quiet. I tiptoed from the room. Halfway down the hall, I tripped on a pile of books stacked near the wall and almost pitched headfirst down the stairs. I caught my balance and froze. The line under Mom and Dad's door remained dark.

I steadied my breathing and crept downstairs and out the front door, easing it closed behind me. For a moment, I stood under the porch light with kamikaze moths trying to dive-bomb my ears. At the curb, the BMW was idling under a streetlamp, with Becca and Kelly in the front seat.

"Hi. You do know it's two thirty a.m.,

right?" I asked as I climbed in. "Because I just want to make sure you're not trying to pick me up for school. Those hallucinations can come on fast, you know."

Kelly twisted around and fixed me with a piercing stare. "Shh. No talking." She pulled up the hood of her sweatshirt and faced forward again, as Becca gunned the engine, jolting us all back against our seats.

"Becca! What is going on?" I yelled as she screeched up the street. "Have you guys gone out of your minds? I've had a really crappy day, as you might remember, and I'd really like to just—"

Kelly twisted around again, this time holding a sweatband in her hands. "For your information, Val, you're being kidnapped. If you keep talking, I'll have to blindfold and gag you." She flourished the piece of terry cloth.

"That's a sweatband," I pointed out.

She looked down. "Yeah, I know." She stuffed it under her seat.

Becca slowed and turned into the Wendy's drive-thru. "Okay, chicks, I think we all need some fuel, because we have a long night ahead of us."

After ordering disgusting amounts of food, Becca drove slowly down side streets and finally pulled into the deep shadows of an oak tree. She rolled down the windows, then sat back with a sigh. The cool night air, scented with damp leaves and earth, blew through the car. I leaned over the center console as Kelly dipped into the big warm paper bag and doled out sandwiches in shiny foil.

I balanced my fries on the seat next to me and unwrapped my Crispy Chicken Deluxe, complete with double bacon, cheese, and extra mayo. The car was quiet except for the sound of thoughtful chewing.

After a few minutes, I stuffed the rest of my sandwich back into the bag and leaned forward. "All right, are you going to tell me what's going on?" I said.

Becca and Kelly glanced at each other. Then Kelly set her half-eaten burger on the dashboard and took a deep breath. She scooted her seat back and faced me. "Look, Val. It's very simple: We're calling off the GNBP."

"What!"

Kelly pulled a piece of grubby folded paper from her back pocket. Maple syrup stains dotted the outside.

"What are you doing with the contract, Kel?" I asked with trepidation.

Kelly glanced at Becca, who nodded slightly. "This . . ." She ripped the paper in half and in half again until my GNBP was reduced to little bits that fluttered over the sidewalk like white moths in the night.

"Stop!" I swiped at the pieces, but they had already scattered.

Becca leaned over. "Look, Val, we think this whole thing has gotten out of control. I mean, at first it was fun, right? With the bet and everything. But lately . . . things have gotten serious. You were really upset when you called me earlier, weren't you?"

I nodded slowly. There was no use in denying it.

Becca went on. "I really did think the GNBP would be good for you, to clear your mind after Dave. And Kelly thought that meeting guys and having a good time would be best for you. Things just got out of control." She opened her car door. "We want you to know we're serious."

Kelly got out of the car too, and after a moment's hesitation, I followed. Becca opened the trunk of the car and hauled out a large mass of something. I peered at it in the dim light. I almost gasped. "It's the dress!"

"And the heels," Kelly chimed in solemnly.

Ceremoniously, Becca marched over to a row of trash cans sitting outside one of the suburban homes nearby. She opened the lid and threw the dress and shoes in. I watched in stunned silence.

"And I told my dad to put the jewels back in the safe-deposit box. No one's wearing them now."

I sank down onto the cool dewy grass. Kelly and Becca each sat down next to me.

"Val." Kelly put her hand on my knee. "Becs and I want to help you. So we're going to interfere in your life one more time." She looked right into my eyes. "You need to tell Adam exactly what you feel and what's been going on."

I was silent. She and Becca watched me anxiously.

Tell Adam everything . . . ? I thought of his hurt face today at the mural and slowly shook my head. He'd never speak to me again. I got to my feet and brushed the damp grass from the rear of my jeans. "This is a lot to digest. I'll think about it, okay?"

They both stood up too. "Val," Becca said.

"That's the other part of our plan. The first part is that we're squashing the GNBP. No more betting, no more games—from any of us. The second part is that we're not letting you go until you swear that you'll talk to Adam. Kelly and I love you—we're not going to let you throw this chance away."

I stared at the earnest faces of my two friends for a long moment. What they had done was nosy and pushy. But it was true—they loved me. Maybe I should trust them on this one. I nodded slowly. "I can't say one hundred percent what I'm going to do. But I hear what you're saying. I really do. I'll think about it, okay?"

"Okay," Becca agreed. "I guess that's all we can really expect."

We drove home through the silent, sleeping streets. As I opened the car door in front of my house, Becca leaned over into the space between the seats, her worried face illuminated by the yellow overhead light. "Val, are you okay? You know this only happened because we love you, right?" she asked.

I gave her a little smile, my first since this afternoon. "Yeah. I don't know what I'm going to do about Adam, but I do know that." I shut the car door and went into the house.

Seventeen

I thought I'd be awake all that night, but after shedding my track pants and cap, I fell into bed and was instantly asleep. When my eyes opened, lemon sunlight was flooding the room and the clock said 7:00. I rubbed my face with both hands. Adam. I had to decide what to do about Adam.

I sat there in bed for an hour, the covers pooling around my waist, arms clasped around my drawn-up knees, letting all the thoughts rattle around in my brain. I could feel the pieces clicking into place, one by one. Before I even realized it, my mind was made up.

I got out of bed. A soft spring breeze stirred the curtains, carrying the scent of honeysuckle from outside, but I barely noticed. I felt like I was following a mental checklist—when it was complete, I'd have fixed my love life or ruined it. There wasn't a lot of middle ground.

First, I grabbed my phone and texted Adam. *Meet me at Brandt Park at 10. Please.* I could only hope he would show up. Then I stripped off my rumpled pajamas and climbed into the shower. The sharp citrus scent of my grapefruit body wash cut any fog left from the night and cleared my head. I pulled on a black cotton sundress and twisted my hair into a knot on top of my head.

When I pulled up to the park entrance, I could already see Adam sitting at a wooden picnic table set in a grove of trees. He was facing away from me, the flickering light from the leaves overhead playing across his shoulders and back. His shoulders were hunched, his hands laced together on the table in front of him.

"Adam," I said quietly as I approached. "Hi." He looked up, stone-faced. I took a deep breath and tentatively perched across from him, the warm wood of the picnic bench splintery under my thighs. He was gazing determinedly at a line of trees in front of us. "Adam, we have to talk," I said. I wanted my voice to come out quiet and firm, but it really sounded more wavery and scared.

He stared at me and said nothing. I dropped my eyes. Whatever happened, Becca and Kelly were right. I had to get this all out. "Adam, I haven't been totally straight with you all these weeks, and I'm really sorry." He lifted one eyebrow but otherwise didn't change expression. "I know there's some serious chemistry between us. I feel it too."

"Well, I *did* think that." He stressed the past tense. I put my hand on the table between us.

"There's something I have to tell you." My words hung in the air before I rushed on. "Ever since before I met you, I've been running this . . . experiment. It was nothing, just something to help me personally. But the plan has been not to go out with anyone, or flirt with anyone, or do anything romantic at all. With any guy . . . including you." I stopped the onslaught of words to take a breath. My eyes were fixed on his face, which was expressionless except for the twitch of a muscle at the corner of his mouth.

I went on. "That's why I couldn't take the coffee that first day. I'm not really allergic. But I thought . . . maybe you were starting to like me a little, and that would mess up my plan. And the same thing with the dance lesson. I really wanted to go with you. But I couldn't—so I asked my cousin Larry to be my partner." I finished, slightly out of breath. I stared down at the splintery wood of the table, where two ants were dragging away a dead wasp.

I could hear Adam's breath whistling in and out. For what seemed like a very long time, he was quiet. Then he spoke. "So you were just playing games this whole time?" His voice was cold.

"No!" I resisted the urge to jump up from the bench and instead leaned across the table. "Adam." I spoke quietly, intently. "It wasn't just a game. This was something I really felt like I needed to do. Things were really hard after Dave and I split up. I just felt like I needed a break from guys. But then things got out of control. I wanted to stop it, but I couldn't." I felt tears prickling behind my eyes.

"But you've basically been lying to me the whole time I've known you."

"I wasn't lying!"

"Well, you weren't being honest. You were covering this up the whole time."

I couldn't stand that quiet iciness. "I couldn't say anything—the rules were that the plan was in place for one month."

"So?" he asked. "What does it matter what the rules were?" He stared at me fiercely. "Why didn't you just forget it?"

"I—I wanted to," I stammered. "But the rules—"

"You already said that." He rose from the bench and walked a few feet away to a battered charcoal grill sitting on a concrete pillar. He stood with his back to me, scraping his fingers across the top. Then he wheeled around. "Why are these rules so important to you?" he demanded. "You're okay just sacrificing real life for rules, no matter what?"

I stood up. "I'm not sacrificing *real life*, whatever that means. I'm just not a quitter— not this, not *anything*." My voice rose. "What I start, I finish, no matter what."

For a long moment we faced each other. Adam's face was red. Then he shook his head. His face closed down. "Forget this. I'm not interested in going out with a liar."

The blood rushed to my face. I could feel a pulse pounding in my forehead. "Well, *I* don't want to be with some sanctimonious, judgmental jerk who criticizes people he doesn't even understand!" My voice rang in the rich green stillness of the park.

Adam shook his head. "See you, Val." He lifted his hand and, without waiting for a response, turned and walked away.

I watched his figure retreat across the grass and climb into the Volvo. The engine started and I could hear the scrape of the tailpipe as he backed out of the parking lot and roared away. Then, with the silence of the park settling around me, I sank back onto the picnic bench and dropped my head into my hands.

My life turned sort of gray after the big blow-out. I went straight home with Becca every day after school. But the afternoons were so empty without Sternwell's. For the first time in my life, all my homework was done ahead of time. I avoided the art hallway like the plague. Once, a couple of days after the fight, I heard Adam's voice nearby while I was at my locker. I darted into the girls' bathroom next to me and held the door open a crack.

He passed by, pale and drawn. The blond girl from the dance lesson was talking to him, but he didn't really seem to be responding.

The only upside I could find, really, was that the guys at school had finally lost interest in the newly single, who was now the oldly single, Val. The Facebook postings and texts had dwindled one by one. Willy started hanging out with a girl in Science Olympiad. Even my faithful Kevin had forgotten me once track season started.

Becca and Kelly tried to cheer me up as much as possible—making me eat giant amounts of junk food, insisting we all cut class one afternoon and go to the water park—but they were mostly consumed by prom preparations: dress shopping, hair consultations, long debates about the pros and cons of strapless. I had already told them I wasn't going. They didn't need to ask why.

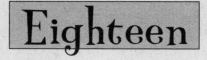

Eighteen

"Are you sure you're going to be okay, honey?" Mom paused in the doorway of the den for the fourth time, eyeing me slumped on the couch in my gray sweatpants. "I just don't feel right about leaving you alone on prom night."

I looked up from *27 Dresses.* "Mom, I'm fine. I swear. Please, go out, have a good time."

"Dad and I would be happy to stay in, honey. We could all play Monopoly."

I groaned silently. "No, Mom, thanks. I'm just going to hang out. It's all good, okay?" I mustered up a convincingly cheerful smile. She wavered in the doorway for a moment.

"Well, only if you're sure . . ."

"I am. Bye! Have a good time at the opera." I waved. Sitting at home on prom night wearing stained sweatpants was just about the pits of my life, but sitting at home on prom night *with my parents* would be absolutely rock bottom.

The front door slammed. I went limp with relief. Now I could just shamelessly wallow. I picked up the remote, aimed it deliberately at the TV, and clicked it off.

For a minute, I sat staring at the blank screen. The house was silent except for the ticking of the kitchen wall clock. I wondered what everyone was doing at prom right then. They'd probably all finished dinner and were just getting to the Belton in the limos. I shook my head. Forget it. Forget prom, school, the GNBP. *Adam,* my brain helpfully reminded me. Especially forget him. I hoisted myself up from the sofa and wandered into the kitchen, pulling open the fridge door. I leaned on it, staring sightlessly into the depths.

Depressing leftovers in Tupperware. Milk. Brita pitcher of water. Eggs. Half a lemon in a plastic bag. Half an onion. Withered strawberries. I heaved a gusty sigh and turned to the pantry, finally pulling out a half-eaten bag of cheddar Goldfish.

I schlumped back to my lair and once again ensconced myself on the couch. I clicked Katherine Heigl back on and lined up a few Goldfish on my stomach, carefully turning them so they were all facing the same way.

My phone buzzed on the coffee table. I glanced at it in a desultory way. Becca.

"Hi."

"Hey there!" She sounded breathless. I could hear the thump of music in the background. "Kels and I wanted to see how you were doing."

I stuck a Goldfish in my mouth. "Awesome. I'm just hanging out. Watching *27 Dresses*. You know, the one where Katherine Heigl's a bridesmaid like a hundred times?"

"We're worried about you, Val! It doesn't feel right to be off here while you're sitting at home," Becca said. "Maybe we should—"

"I'm fine." I cut her off. "Seriously, I'm good. You know, just relaxing. You guys have fun, okay?" I forced a bit of bubbly into my voice. "Call me tomorrow and tell me all about it, okay?"

"Okay." She sounded doubtful. I could

hear a male voice talking in the background. She said something indistinct back. Then she returned to the phone. "Logan wants to go dance."

"Go! Text me later, okay?" I clicked the phone off and lay back against the pillows. Being upbeat was exhausting.

A half hour later, I'd almost made it to the bottom of the Goldfish bag when the doorbell rang. I paused the movie and, still clutching the crackers, heaved myself off the couch.

I could only see a shadowy figure behind the frosted glass. Probably just an ax murderer looking for girls who stay home on prom night. Good. I could use a little excitement. I flicked on the porch light and opened the door.

Adam stood there in front of me, wearing a slim-cut black tux and holding a giant pink rose wrist corsage. My mouth dropped open. He extended the flowers toward me.

"Please don't close the door. I have to talk to you," he said, talking very fast. "That day in the park was a total mess. I'm an idiot."

I stood frozen to the spot, one hand on the door, the other still clutching my nearly empty bag of Goldfish.

Adam kept talking. "I was just upset—I felt hurt but I didn't say it very well. I'm so sorry. I'm glad you were finally honest with me. I knew the minute I got in the car what a mistake it was leaving you in the park like that. Have I totally messed this up, or do I still have a chance?"

Gingerly, I released my hold on the door. I felt like I had to move carefully or I might topple over. I looked around me for a place to put the Goldfish bag. There wasn't anywhere. Adam saw what I was trying to do. He extended his hand and I placed the bag in it. Now he had the corsage in one hand and the Goldfish bag in the other. I opened my mouth. "I . . . I . . ." I couldn't get any other words past my numb lips.

Adam's face fell. Then he nodded slowly. "Okay. I understand. I just felt like I had to try, you know?" He turned and walked back down the porch steps. He had almost reached the door of his car before I realized what he was doing.

"Wait, Adam, wait!" I sprang forward as if shot out of a starting gate. Clattering down the steps, I ran over to the car and grabbed him by the sleeve. "Don't leave! I was just trying to understand how this could be happening. To be honest, I thought I'd ruined things between us forever with the stupid No-Boyfriend Plan. I'm so, so happy you're not mad. And I'm so sorry I almost messed everything up between you and me."

Adam's face lit up. He set the Goldfish bag on top of the car. "Okay. Well then, do you want to go to prom? I know it's kind of short notice—"

"Yes!" I shouted. I threw my arms around his neck, almost knocking him over. He staggered and caught himself against the car.

"Okay," he said, grinning. Gently, he disentangled my arms from around his neck and slipped the corsage over my wrist. The pink rosebuds were heavy and fragrant on my wrist. I raised my arm and buried my nose in the delicate blooms. Adam was digging something out of the backseat of the car. Before I had time to wonder what he was doing, he turned around. Floating from his hands was the dark blue silk gown I'd seen in his house. I gaped at him. He smiled shyly. "My mom said you could borrow it tonight. She said she thought my grandmother would have loved this story.

I thought maybe since this is kind of short notice, you might not have a dress already."

I took the gown. The blue silk slid through my hands like water. "I'll be right back."

Up in my room, I nervously slid the dress over my head and smoothed the fabric. It fell perfectly over my hips, just brushing the tips of my toes. Quickly, I slipped on my high-heeled silver sandals and brushed my hair satiny-smooth, pulling it back into a loose, low bun at the back of my neck. I slicked on a little raspberry lip stain on my mouth and brushed my lashes with jet-black mascara. Then I opened my bedroom door and took a deep breath. I peered over the landing. Adam was pacing around below. I steadied myself on the high heels and carefully made my way down the stairs.

Adam looked up at my approach. His eyes widened. "Wow," he said. "I don't think that dress looked like that on my grandmother."

"Thanks, I think," I replied, trying not to clutch the banister for balance. I didn't wear heels that often. "So should we go?"

"Yeah." He opened the front door. "We just have to make one quick stop first."

Halfway through the ride to the Belton Banquet Club, I sat up in my seat. Something was missing. I couldn't quite place what it was, but the car seemed different somehow. Then it hit me—the screech was gone. I looked at Adam. "You fixed the tailpipe!"

He glanced over and smiled. "I was wondering when you'd notice."

"Aww, I kind of miss it," I said. He slowed down. I looked out the window. "This isn't the way to the Belton."

"I know. I just have to pick something up at a buddy's house first." We were driving down an unfamiliar street with regal houses spaced widely apart. Adam peered through the windshield. "I think this is it." He turned into a driveway, but instead of stopping at the house, he continued right past it. The driveway kept going, past the back lawn and into a little grove of trees. He stopped the car and killed the engine.

I looked around. It was totally black among the trees, though I could just make out the yellow lights of the house through the branches. Adam came around and opened my door.

"You left something out *here*?" I asked, stepping from the car and concentrating on keeping my heirloom silk hem out from under my heels. I had a feeling Adam's mom might appreciate that.

"Yeah." He grabbed my hand and started pulling me through the grove. "It's through here."

"Adam!" I ducked a low-hanging branch. Leaves brushed my face. "What's going—" I stopped suddenly as the trees gave way to an open clearing, filled with flower beds and little grass paths, illuminated by the light of the moon. "It's the Shakespeare garden." I twisted and looked up at Adam, who was watching me with a huge grin. "What's . . . ? How did we . . . ?"

"Remember I told you my dad was the owner's contractor? Well, I asked him if we could come here for a bit. We just came in the front way, instead of through Kelly's property." He reached behind a gray rock nearby and pulled out a big plastic basket. I squinted at it. "Is that a laundry basket?"

"Yeah." He pulled out a green wool blanket and laid it out on the grass. "I know when you take a girl on a romantic picnic, you should have a wicker basket or something, but this was all I could find."

"A romantic picnic," I breathed as I sank

down on the blanket. I realized I wasn't sounding super-intelligent, but things were moving awfully fast. One minute I'm at home wallowing in sweatpants, the next, I'm in a silk dress, having a romantic picnic with a hot guy.

I leaned back on my elbows and inhaled the heavy scent of roses as Adam laid out some little slices of French bread. "This is amazing. How did you get it all here?"

He arranged brownies on a white plate and added a bowl of fresh red raspberries. "It was easy—I just stopped by and dropped off the basket right before I went to your house. I figured if you turned me down, I'd just come back and eat it all myself."

I giggled. "So I have to know," I said after a little pause. "What made you change your mind about, er, us?"

"Do you really want to know?" He pulled out a wedge of Brie.

"Of course."

"Well, I actually can't take all the credit," he said. "After that big fight, I just shut down. You know? I tend to do that when I'm upset. Just close myself off. I told myself to forget you, that it wasn't worth it, you'd lied to me—"

"Okay, yeah, I get it." I rolled my eyes.

"Do I have to relive it right now?"

"Sorry. Anyway, I'm telling you this because it was a really stupid thing for me to do. But the worst part was that it was working. I just threw myself into school and painting, and after a few days, I wasn't obsessing over you as much. But I wasn't happy—I was miserable, actually."

I put my hand over his and he smiled at me.

"Anyway, I don't even know what would have happened if Becca and Kelly—"

"What!"

"—hadn't called me last night."

I shook my head. "They actually called you?"

"Yeah. And they put me on speaker and basically told me that you were crazy about me and how sad you'd been ever since our fight."

I could feel my cheeks growing pink. He grinned a little wickedly.

"It's not that I *wanted* you to be upset—"

"No, of course not," I teased.

"But it did show me that you cared. So I asked them if they thought you would ever forgive me. And they said they thought you would." He smiled right into my eyes.

"And last but not least . . ." He pulled out a bottle of sparkling cider, the sides frosty and beaded with moisture, and twisted the wire cap. I squealed as the cork popped and the cider ran foaming from the top and down the sides. Adam poured some into two flutes, his fingers lingering on mine as he handed me one.

"Thanks," I said. I knew my voice had gone husky. Suddenly it was hard to look him in the face. Instead, I stared down at my silk-draped lap.

Adam lifted his glass. "Here's . . . to dumb mistakes."

I looked up. His icy blue eyes were smiling at me. I raised my own glass. "To dumb mistakes."

Nineteen

As Adam and I stepped into the dim, twin-kling interior of the Belton, I caught my breath. The dance floor was packed with girls in long, elaborate dresses and guys in tuxes. Black Eyed Peas blared from the speakers. Strings of lights were strung everywhere and red silk hung in folds from the ceiling and dripped down the walls, giv-ing the room the feel of a desert tent. The tables scattered around the perimeter of the dance floor were draped in orange table-cloths and set with huge bouquets of yellow and red gerbera daisies.

"Val!"

A blur of violet rushed toward me. Adam and I stopped inside the front doors just as the blur barreled up to us. It was Becca, wearing a skintight dress that appeared to be made entirely of Lycra. Kelly, clad in a long black sheath, was close behind. They skidded to a halt in front of us, breathless. Brent and Logan followed behind.

"Hi, girls," I said casually. "*27 Dresses* was boring, so I thought I'd try prom. Good idea, huh?" I took Adam's arm.

My friends looked from Adam's beaming face to my own and back again. Kelly nodded slowly. "Excellent idea. Probably you got that from some very smart people, right?"

I shrugged. "Just some girls I know." Kelly laughed.

"Val, you look amazing," Becca said, examining a fold of my dress. "What is this, vintage?"

I glanced at Adam. "I guess you could say that."

Just then, the music behind me shifted to "Beat It" and people started screaming and jumping up and down. "Oh my God," Becca squealed, grabbing Kelly and me by the hands. "Come on!"

All six of us crowded onto the dance floor, sweating, bumping against people, everyone shouting the words. I raised my arms above my head and swayed to the music. I hadn't felt so free since——well, since before spring break. Suddenly, I felt someone grab me around the waist from behind. I shrieked as Adam lifted me high in the air and twirled me so fast my skirt flew out like a giant pinwheel.

"Adam!" I yelled, beating on his back. "Put me down! I'm flashing the whole school!"

"Is that a problem?" he yelled back, still twirling.

"Well, I'm going to barf down your back, how about that?"

He stopped short and set me on my feet. I doubled over, laughing so hard I thought I really might barf.

Suddenly I felt an elbow in my side. "Val, check it out," Becca said, nodding her head toward the front of the dance floor. There was Taylor, wearing a strapless orange minidress that she was practically falling out of, and dancing with Kevin, if what they were doing could actually be called dancing——it was more like vertical making out. She was either overcome by his presence or drunk because her eyes were half-closed and she was dragging in his arms. I had the distinct sense that if he were to let her go, she would have fallen in a heap on the floor.

"Where's Dave?" We scanned the room.

"There he is." Becca pointed to a table in the corner where Dave was slouched, staring fixedly at Taylor and Kevin. Then, as we watched, he slammed his hand on the table and got up.

"Oh, this is going to be good!" Becca squealed, hanging on to my arm. I clutched her back and we giggled as Dave stalked up to the front of the room. The blasting music made it too hard to hear them, but we didn't need to. Dave tapped Taylor on the shoulder and she whirled around, suddenly wide awake. We could see her scream at him, gesturing toward Kevin, who was standing there looking self-satisfied, and then Dave shouted back. This went on for quite a while until she finally grabbed Kevin's hand and the two flounced off toward the doors.

I looked at Becca. She looked at me, and then at the same time, we yelled "Yeah!" and slapped hands.

"Hey, guys." Kelly panted up to us. "We're going to go hang out on the golf course. Do you want to come?"

"Sure," Becca said.

Adam and I looked at each other. Then Adam shook his head. "No, I think we'll stay here and dance some more," he said. Just then, the lights went down and the DJ put on Lady Antebellum's "I Run to You." The first chords began as Adam took my hand and pulled me toward the dance floor, wrapping his arms around me.

The music filled the vast dark room. The other dancers were only shadows. Silver flashes from the ball overhead flew by as I rested my head on Adam's warm chest and closed my eyes. I sensed him lean down, and as if by instinct, I lifted my face toward his. This time, neither of us turned away. His lips were warm and firm as he kissed me once, lightly. I clasped my hands at the back of his neck. He held me against him and pressed his lips to mine again. After an eternity, I looked up at his sparkling eyes. "Are you going to run away from me now?" he teased.

I shook my head, grinning. "No. You can even make me a coffee if you want."

He laughed and pulled me closer as we swayed to the music swirling around us.

Epilogue

The sun shone on my shoulders as I got out of the car at Sternwell's the next day. Adam and I just had a few touches left on the mural. When I rounded the corner to our spot, I stopped short and laughed. There, sitting on the grass, was Adam, and next to him steamed a big cup topped with fluffy whipped cream. "Is that for me?" I asked, pointing at the coffee.

"Maybe," he said, his eyes crinkling at the corners. "Are you sure you're not going to swell up with hives?"

I grinned. "Well, if I did, you'd be here to take care of me, right?"

"Definitely." He handed me the coffee.

For the last time, we poured out the

paint and, shuffling on our knees, finished the section we had abandoned the day of our big fight. Adam stretched and cracked his back as I painted the final stroke of blue in the corner. With a sigh, I dunked my brush in the water bucket and sank down on the warm grass next to Adam. In front of us, the colors of the mural shone like a gorgeous fan spread over the wall.

"I can't believe it's finished," Adam said, draping his arm around my shoulders. I leaned into him.

"It's not," I said. He looked at me in surprise.

I smiled and took his hand. "It's only the beginning."

About the Author

Emma Carlson Berne lives in Cincinnati, Ohio, with her husband, Aaron; son, Henry; and misbehaving yet eternally faithful dog, Holly.

LOL at this sneak peek of

At First Sight
By Catherine Hapka

A new Romantic Comedy from Simon Pulse

⭐

My best friend, Britt, was madly in love. Again.

"OMG!" she said with an adorable giggle, fluttering her long eyelashes at the cute guy in the kung fu T-shirt and Abercrombie cargoes. "I can't believe you go to Greenleaf High. I've always said Greenleaf has the cutest guys in the entire state of Maryland. Right, Lauren?" She waved one hand in my direction without breaking eye contact with Greenleaf Guy. "By the way, this is my best friend, Lauren Foley."

My introduction barely warranted a cursory glance, nod, and mumbled "hi" from the object of Britt's affection. Or maybe that should be "affliction." See, Britt has a lifelong case of severe boycrazyitis. One I seriously doubted would be cured anytime soon.

"Lauren's the one who convinced me to come over and say hi to you," Britt continued, tilting her head up at Greenleaf Guy.

"Usually I'm totally shy about talking to cute guys."

It was all I could do not to burst out laughing at that one. Britt, shy with guys? Hardly. She's pretty much fearless, not to mention completely lacking in the capacity for shame or embarrassment. Everyone says that's why guys are drawn to her like dogs to a fire hydrant. Not that she isn't cute—she is. But even if a guy doesn't notice her pixielike face, her perfect skin, or her great legs, she makes damn sure he notices *her*.

To keep from blowing her cover, I wandered off a ways and pretended to be fascinated by a display case showing an astronaut in full bubble-headed regalia. Britt and I, along with the rest of the junior class of Potomac Point High and those of like half the other schools in our county, were at the National Air and Space Museum at the Smithsonian in Washington, D.C. Why, you ask? Good question. The answer is, we were being subjected to a ridiculously lame multischool field trip sponsored by some science foundation.

Not that I have anything against the Smithsonian. In fact, I kinda like it, especially the First Ladies' gowns at the American History museum. But spaceships and black holes and airplanes? So not my thing.

I watched Britt and the guy in the reflection of the display case. I saw her toss her short blond hair around—a patented Britt flirting move. It worked. The guy stepped a little closer, his hands twitching as if he was dying to touch her.

Then I saw Britt glance around with an adorably furtive expression. She reached into her purse and pulled out BBB. That's a nickname I came up with; it stands for Beloved BlackBerry. It could just as easily stand for Britt's Bodacious Bestie, BlackBerry Baby, or Beautiful Best Buddy. Get the picture? She loves the thing.

Anyway, PDAs, cell phones, and all other electronic devices were strictly verboten on this trip, but Britt has never been that good at following the rules. One of the numerous things she and I *don't* have in common. So she and the guy bent over the BlackBerry, her slim fingers flying over the tiny keys.

My gaze drifted away. I knew what came next. Britt would enter the guy's name and number into her log, then add him as a friend on Facebook. I wondered if he'd be shocked when he logged on and saw that his "shy" new acquaintance had like forty gazillion other FB friends, mostly guys. . . .

As I amused myself with that thought, I found myself staring at the spaceman in front of me. The bubble-headed look was a little retro for my taste. I automatically started redesigning the space suit, adding a touch of color here, streamlining the fabric there . . .

See, that's my thing. Fashion. I love clothes. Most of my daydreams revolve around becoming an international fashion icon, showing up on runways from New York to Milan with my daringly original designs, shocking and amazing the fashion elite with my talent and creativity.

Not that I would ever have the guts to actually *do* anything like that. Britt is always on my case about being too cautious. She wants me to actually create every over-the-top outfit I sketch, no matter how wild or weird, and then wear it to school just to see what happens. But unlike her, I'm not a just-to-see-what-happens kind of girl. I prefer to test the waters first.

My gaze returned to the reflective surface of the display case, but this time I was staring at myself. My ordinary hazel eyes. My perky but unexceptional nose. And my best feature, my long, thick, wavy dark hair. If I ever tried shaking it around like Britt did with hers, would it have the same mesmerizing effect on guys? Or would I just end up looking like I had a gnat in my ear? Thoughts like that never seemed to occur to Britt at all, but my brain produced them so freely that I sometimes wondered if it was a medically diagnosable condition.

"Listen up, people!" Mr. Feldman's voice rang out across the museum. He's the head of PPH's science department and actually a pretty cool guy, despite teaching my least favorite subject and being possibly the worst-dressed high school teacher of all time. And if you've ever been to high school, you know that's saying something. "It's time for a fascinating look at the work scientists do behind the scenes here at the Air and Space Museum," he said in his nasal voice. "Potomac Point and East Elm students, please come with me. March!"

A couple of other teachers called out similar orders, directing the other schools to their own areas. The horde of high schoolers filling the museum's airy atrium started dividing itself into smaller groups like some giant amoeba splitting into different parts, and I started preparing myself for more tedium. See, wandering around on guided tours of the museum's endless array of flying machines, as boring as it was, was actually the fun part. In between, we were stuck listening to a bunch of lectures about stuff like quarks and wind shear and who knew what else. Speaking as someone who can barely stay awake in science class, I couldn't think of a suckier way to spend my day.

Britt bounced over to join me as I started shuffling along with the crowd following Mr. Feldman. "What did you think of Trent?" she demanded eagerly. "Isn't he the awesomest? Talk about love at first sight!"

"Sort of like the other three guys you've fallen in love with so far today?" I paused, feigning deep thought with one finger to my chin. "Or was it four? I've lost count."

"Mock me if you wish, Lauren," she retorted. "Trent might very well be the love of my life. I would hope my best friend might at least *try* to be happy for me."

"If you make it to your two-week anniversary with that guy, I'll be ecstatic, trust me," I told her as we filed into some backstage part of the museum. "Not to mention shocked."

Britt stuck out her tongue at me. We had to stop talking for a while as some dude started droning on about the scientific method. Or something like that. I had to mentally redesign not only his wardrobe—I put him in classic dark pinstripes with a floral tie for a splash of color—but also those of everyone else in the room just to keep from dozing off.

Seventeen hours later, we were finally released back into the main part of the museum. Okay, maybe it wasn't quite that long. But it felt like it. Most of the other schools hadn't yet emerged from their torture chambers—er, lectures—so the place had a weekday-morning-at-the-mall sort of feel. Not that I'd ever have the guts to skip class to go shopping, of course.

"So are you saying you don't believe Trent and I are meant to be?" Britt asked, picking up right where we'd left off.

"I'm saying I don't believe in love at first sight." We'd had this same discussion so many times it was practically scripted. "There's no way you can tell if you're going to hit it off with someone just by looking at him."

"Trust me, babe. I can tell."

Britt sank down onto a free bench, casting an appraising eye toward a good-looking artsy type standing nearby looking at one of the displays. When a Goth girl with a nose ring came over and wrapped one skinny arm around him, stretching up to lick his earlobe, Britt shrugged and returned her gaze to me.

"It's called sparks," she informed me. "And I know them when I feel them."

"Right. *Every* time you feel them." I smirked. "And sorry, but I'm just not willing to believe that sparks and raw animal attraction equal true love."

She grinned back at me. "Don't knock it till you try it. Your love life could stand a little more raw animal attraction."

"If you say so." It was a familiar exchange. Britt wasn't trying to be mean about my love life—or relative lack thereof. I knew she truly didn't understand how I could be content waiting for romance to come to me rather than rushing out, grabbing it with both hands, and checking out its butt, like she did.

But that was mutual. I didn't really get the whole "sparks" thing, either. I mean, sure, I sometimes felt a flutter of hormones when I saw a cute guy walking through the mall or something. Same flutter I got when I saw a hot actor on TV or up on the movie screen. That silly flutter just didn't seem like a solid basis for a relationship to me.

One of the other school groups emerged from their lecture. A pair of beefy jock types wearing varsity jackets wandered past where we were sitting, ribbing each other loudly about football. Or maybe baseball. Something with balls, anyway. Britt sized them up as they passed our bench.

"Any sparks?" I teased.

She tore her gaze away from the guys and made a face at me. "Very funny. You know I'm totally committed to Trent."

For about two and a half seconds she managed to keep a straight face. Then she cracked up. So did I.

"Seriously, though, Lauren," she said, once we got control of ourselves, "I wish you'd let yourself go and just believe in love for a change."

"I do believe in love. Just not love at first sight."

"Okay. But why not at least give the sparks thing a try? What could it hurt?"

"Oh, I don't know. Dying of embarrassment probably hurts at least a little bit."

"You wouldn't actually die, you know," she said.

"I know. I'd just *want* to. And then I'd have to go into the witness protection program, and I'd probably end up living in, like, Iowa or somewhere, with a family who eats mac and cheese for dinner every night and wears polyester. And that would be truly painful."

"Very creative," she said. "But you're avoiding the question. Why not try it just once?"

"That's not the point. I'm not like you. I don't get sparks."

"You say it like it's a disease, Ms. Uptight."

"I'm not uptight. Just sane," I shot back automatically.

She gave me a look. As usual every thought in her head was written all over her face, and I knew she didn't really believe me. She thought I was just holding back, not letting myself go for it with guys the way she did. But it wasn't like that. I truly didn't get the sparks she was always claiming to feel with Mr. Right—du-Jour. Or du-Hour. It just hadn't worked for me like that in the past. I'd only had a couple of semi-serious boyfriends in my entire life, and in both cases they'd started out as friendships that slowly grew into more.

"Look, you deal with guys and romance and stuff your way, and I deal with it in mine," I told her.

"You mean Jason and that guy from the pool?" She wrinkled her nose. "Please. Hanging out with a guy for ages until one night you stay up too late watching scary movies and accidentally start making out hardly qualifies as romance."

She made it sound so sordid. And worse yet, so dull.

"Jason and I were together for almost six months," I reminded her.

"And then what happened? Things got boring and fizzled out. Real romantic."

"It still beats your two-week record for a relationship lasting," I retorted.

She grinned. "Okay, touché or whatever. But listen, seriously? This trip is the perfect time to scope out some fresh meat. There are tons of cute guys here from other schools, so if you do embarrass yourself, you'll never have to see them again. But it's way more likely they'll be so blown away by your gorgeous face, superhot bod, and incredible hair that you'll end up with more dates than me."

"If I do, I'll probably end up in *Guinness World Records*."

"Come on, I'm serious." Britt reached into her purse for her favorite MAC lipstick. "What's the worst that could happen? And it's not like you're all fascinated by this spaceship stuff anyway."

I glanced around at the rocket-type artifacts surrounding us. "True. But I'm happy just to sit here and wallow in boredom. You go ahead and scope away to your heart's content. I'll watch and take notes."

"No you won't." After reapplying, she capped her lipstick and dropped it back in her purse. "You'll just watch, and then make fun of me later."

"You know me so well."

My tone was light, but she responded with uncharacteristic seriousness. "Right. And I know you well enough to know you deserve to find the perfect guy. All it takes is a little effort, a little risk."

"Well, maybe if I ever actually run into someone who's worth the . . ."

My voice trailed off before I could finish the sentence. Because I'd just spotted the most jaw-droppingly gorgeous guy I'd ever seen.

From **WILD** *to* **ROMANTIC**, *don't miss these* **PROM** *stories from Simon Pulse!*

Prama

How I Created My
Perfect Prom Date

Prom Crashers

Fat Hoochie Prom Queen

From Simon Pulse

• • •

Published by Simon & Schuster

Want to hear what the
Romantic Comedies
authors are doing
when they are not
writing books?

Check out
PulseRoCom.com
to see the authors
blogging together,
plus get sneak peeks
of upcoming titles!

SimON TEEN

Simon & Schuster's **Simon Teen**
e-newsletter delivers current updates
on the hottest titles, exciting
sweepstakes, and exclusive content
from your favorite authors.

Visit **TEEN.SimonandSchuster.com**
to sign up, post your thoughts, and find
out what every avid reader is talking about!

Margaret K. McElderry Books
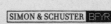
SIMON & SCHUSTER BFYR

SIMON PULSE